The
HIGHBINDERS

Oliver Bleeck

The
HIGHBINDERS

OLIVER BLEECK

PERENNIAL LIBRARY

Harper & Row, Publishers

New York, Cambridge, Philadelphia, San Francisco

London, Mexico City, São Paulo, Singapore, Sydney

First PERENNIAL LIBRARY edition published 1984.

Library of Congress Cataloging in Publication Data

Bleeck, Oliver, 1926–
  The highbinders.

  Reprint. Originally published: New York : Morrow, c1974.
  I. Title.
PS3570.H58H5 1984   813'.54   83-48946
ISBN 0-06-080702-4 (pbk.)

84 85 86 87 88 10 9 8 7 6 5 4 3 2 1

Chapter One

*T*he carnation made me feel silly. It was supposed to be red, but the flower shop in the Hilton had only pink ones so I paid fifteen pence for one and let the girl in the shop pin it to my lapel.

"My, don't we look nice," she said. "Like to use our mirror?"

"I seem to remember how I look," I said, smiled my good-bye, and crossed the lobby, heading for the hotel entrance and a taxi. Nobody noticed my carnation and I think I felt a trifle disappointed.

It was 5:35 P.M. and the London traffic rush was on, but for only twenty pence the Hilton doorman whistled me up a taxi, held the door for me, inquired of my destination, and after I told him, repeated it to the driver, "The Black Thistle on New Cavendish Street. Know it, mate?"

"I should hope to," the driver said, gave the meter flag a twist, and nosed his cab out into the Park Lane traffic.

It wasn't much of a ride, not more than three-quarters of a mile, if that, but the traffic was thick and stubborn

1

and we didn't pull up in front of the Black Thistle until nearly six o'clock.

I've never much cared for pubs. I suppose it's because I detest cocktail parties and an English pub, right after five-thirty opening time, reminds me of nothing so much as an American cocktail party that's about to run out of gin.

The Black Thistle was a Watney pub and it seemed fairly new, or at least its furbishings did, with lots of glittering vinyl and some embarrassingly bad murals on two walls. I made my way through the crowd at the bar, asked for and got a large whisky, poured a little water into it from a pitcher, pocketed the change from a pound, turned, and had the glass knocked from my hand by a gray tweed elbow that was covered with a black suede patch.

The elbow belonged to a man who was holding a pint of beer. His back had been to me and when he turned I saw that he was in his late twenties, a little over six feet tall, and already growing a paunch. He had a smooth plump pink face that was turning red. I think he was blushing.

"Terribly sorry," he said. "Did I get any on you?"

"It's all right," I said.

He bent down to pick up my glass and I got a good view of the top of his head. It was as bald and as pink as his face, except for a thick white scar on his crown that was about two inches long. What hair he had left was light blond and confined to the sides of his head and the nape of his neck. He wore it long and brushed back so that it hung down over the collar of his figured blue shirt.

When he rose he smiled apologetically and said, "What were you drinking, whisky?"

"That's right."

"A large one, I'd think. I'll get you another."

"Don't bother."

He smiled again. His teeth were a bit gray, but it was still a nice enough smile. "If somebody slopped my drink,

2

they could bloody well buy me another. Be back in a second."

It was more like sixty seconds before he could shoulder his way back through the chattering crowd bearing my drink. It even had an ice cube in it. I noticed then that his eyes were a familiar shade of gray and I couldn't remember where I had seen that particular shade recently until he smiled again and I saw his teeth. "American, aren't you?" he said, handing me the drink.

"That's right."

"Thought you might like the ice. Most of you chaps do."

"Thanks."

"Are you all set now?"

"I'm fine."

He smiled his gray smile again. "Well, enjoy yourself."

I nodded and he turned away and moved into the crowd. I moved out of it, edging toward the door where nobody was standing and where anybody who wanted to could admire the carnation in my buttonhole. After I took a swallow of my drink I looked at my watch. It was five past six. I was still ten minutes early.

A large English whisky is about equivalent to a single shot in a fairly honest New York bar so I had quickly finished my drink and was trying to decide whether it was really worth the effort to go for a refill when the cramps hit. They hit just above my belt and it was as if somebody had slammed my stomach with an iron pipe. From the inside.

I doubled over and dropped the empty glass. It rolled a couple of feet. The pain hit again, even worse than before, and this time it was as though iron prongs were digging into my stomach, rusty iron prongs, and I thought wasn't I lucky that Harley Street was only three blocks away. An appendicitis would be only routine to the men of Harley Street—just as it had been to old Dr. Marland who had cut my appendix out the summer that I was fifteen years old.

The pain gave way to nausea, a wave of it, and I knew

3

I was going to throw up. Because I'm basically a tidy sort I decided that it would be better to throw up outside in the gutter rather than all over the Black Thistle's pretty purple carpet.

I turned and lurched toward the door. The pain went away almost as quickly as it had come. In its place was the nausea plus a curious sense of well-being that somehow combined the peace of marijuana with the recklessness of three martinis. But it was better than both. The closest I had ever been to it before was for a fleeting moment once when I had counted backwards from ten while a dentist injected sodium pentothal into my left arm just before hacking out an impacted wisdom tooth. You won't feel a thing, he had said, and I hadn't, except a supreme sense of confident elation.

I felt the same way as I stumbled outside and made a mess in the New Cavendish street gutter, but not really minding at all because I could cope with that and, if given just a few moments' rest, could probably even come up with a passkey to the universe.

But I was never to have the chance. My arms were grabbed from behind. In front of me two men and a girl came out of the Black Thistle. They looked at me. The girl made a face and giggled and the two men grinned and then laughed. I decided not to be mugged, not in broad daylight on New Cavendish Street, London W. 1. Not with a small crowd looking on and grinning and giggling about it.

I jerked my right arm free and drove my elbow back hard. It sank into something soft and I heard a most satisfactory whoosh. A voice said, "Here, now!" so I stamped down hard with my left heel on something that felt very much like an instep. "Get him, Bill!" another voice said. I was all set to spin and kick Bill in the balls when hard hands clamped on my left wrist and thrust it up and back until my own hand was between my shoulder blades. Another slight jerk and my left shoulder would go. I decided that it wasn't worth it and that I should

4

stop struggling and start complaining. "Goddamned bastards," I said.

"Here, now," the first voice said again. "That's no way to talk."

I turned my head and got a look at the one I had hit in the stomach. He had a hard young face with a mean thin mouth and pale blue eyes as friendly as snakes. He also had a set of long blond sideburns. I couldn't see the rest of his hair because he had it covered up with the blue pot helmet that London police constables normally wear.

Chapter
Two

*T*he light bulb was the first thing I saw when I awoke. It was a weak, frosted one, not much more than a sickly twenty-five watts, and it was screwed into a socket in a ceiling that must have been twenty feet high. I assumed that the light never went off, not until it burned out.

I lay there and had the headache. Actually, it was a bit more than a headache. It was a malignant tumor that was going to burst through my skull right above the eyes where the sinuses were. It was, I decided, a rotten way to die.

But instead of dying, I got up. At least I swung my feet down to the floor and raised myself into a slumped sort of sitting position. I had been lying on a slab of yellow tile that was fitted into one corner of the room about two feet above the floor. It was a bed. To soften it up were two gray blankets that felt as though they had been woven out of wooden fiber. Fairly soft wood perhaps. One of the blankets had been folded up and I had used it as a pillow. I didn't remember folding the blanket.

I didn't remember anything after meeting the muggers who had turned out to be two London cops.

They must have brought me to where I was, which, I saw, was a jail cell and a rather spacious one at that. I estimated it to be at least seven feet wide and twelve feet long and apparently designed for single occupancy. Furnishings and appointments other than the tile bunk included a seatless toilet, a one-tap sink, a big gray iron door with a peephole, no windows, and a former occupant's scratched notation that "Lord God it is awful here."

I got up, used the toilet, drank some water from the tap, and reached for a cigarette. I didn't have any. I went through my pockets and there was nothing in them. I looked at my left wrist. My watch was still on it and the time was half past five. In the morning, I assumed. They had let me keep my watch, my clothes, my headache, and my pink carnation. The carnation looked old and tired and bedraggled and I felt that we had a lot in common except that it still smelled nice.

I had never been in jail before. Not to stay. Not in a jail where they slam a big iron door shut on you. I had once spent part of a night in a New York precinct station, but there they had kept me in a room with some desks and some chairs and a window and they had let me keep my cigarettes and my matches and even a little of my dignity.

For what seemed to be a long time I stood there in the middle of the cell and looked around. I decided that I could never do a five-year stretch. Or a five-month one. Or even five days. Five hours were about my limit and I had already done that and more, so I went over and started kicking hell out of the big iron door.

After a while they came to see what was the matter. After a week maybe, or ten days, somebody came and opened the peephole and said, "Stop that kicking now. We got people here who're trying to sleep."

8

"I just thought I'd let you know I'm ready to leave," I said.

"Ready to leave, are we?"

"That's right."

"Sobered up a bit, have we?"

I wasn't going to argue. "Stone sober."

I felt him taking a good look at me through the peephole. Finally, the voice said, "Well, let's see what Sergeant Matthews has got to say." The peephole slammed shut.

It took Sergeant Matthews a fortnight to make up his mind about me. Or maybe it was only ten days. That was jail time. By real time, the time on my watch, it was fifteen minutes before the key clacked and turned in the lock. The big iron door swung open and a young policeman stood there, dangling a large key from a large ring and nodding his head as if I were about what he had expected; certainly no better.

"This way," he said, and I followed him down a hall that was lined with big iron doors like the one I had been behind. We entered a room that held some desks and a wooden bench and some chairs. Behind one of the desks was a policeman with three stripes on his sleeve. Sergeant Matthews, I presumed.

"Here he is, Sergeant, Mr. Philip St. Ives," the young policeman said and the sergeant looked at me with thirty- or thirty-one-year-old green eyes that were neither friendly nor unfriendly and if not incurious, certainly indifferent.

"Sit down, Mr. St. Ives," Sergeant Matthews said.

I sat down and he reached into a drawer and drew out a manila envelope and started removing its contents. The contents were what had been in my pockets. He ticked the items off on a form, shoving them across the desk to me one by one. When he got to the cigarettes I said, "Mind if I smoke?"

"Not at all, sir," he said without looking up.

I lit one of the Pall Malls and blew some smoke up into

9

the air. The cigarette tasted all right, better than I had expected, but it did my headache no good.

"Your people must have been English, a name like that," he said.

"Or French," I said.

"Oh?"

"The French spell it with a Y."

"Pretty little place. St. Ives, I mean. Ever been there?"

"No."

"Pretty little place."

That seemed to exhaust the topic and Sergeant Matthews shoved the last item across the desk to me and said, "Would you count your money, sir? Should be thirty-one pounds and nine pence there plus some American coins."

I counted it and put the money into my wallet. "It's all there."

He nodded. "Sign here, please."

While I signed the form he said, "I must say, I expected you to be a size bigger."

I handed him back his pen. "Why?"

"From the way my men were talking when I came on duty, they claimed to have collared themselves an American karate expert. Constable Wilson especially—limping around he was with a bad foot to prove it."

"I don't know any karate," I said. "I just thought I was being mugged."

"At six o'clock in the evening and the sun not down?" Sergeant Matthews made his brown eyebrows form two skeptical arcs.

"I'd forgotten where I was when they grabbed me."

"Your home's New York, isn't it, sir?"

"That's right."

"I don't suppose they wait until dark there. Muggers, I mean."

"Daylight or dark, it's all pretty much the same to them."

"Must be an interesting place."

"Terribly," I said. "What're you charging me with, drunk and disorderly?"

"Just drunk, sir."

I tapped my wallet with a finger. "Have I got enough in here to cover it?"

"That'll be up to the magistrate, sir."

"Can't I just post bond and forget about it? Forfeit it, I mean."

Sergeant Matthews shook his head. He seemed a little sorry about the entire thing. "Afraid not, sir," he said, handing me an official-looking form. "This is your summons to appear at the Marlborough Street Magistrates' Court at nine this morning."

I sighed, took the summons, folded it, and put it away in a pocket. "What if I don't show?"

All traces of sympathy vanished. "Then a warrant will be issued for your arrest."

"I'll be there," I said. "Can I go now?"

"Certainly, sir." Sergeant Matthews looked at the clock on the wall. "You should be able to get back to your hotel, take a nap, tidy up, get a good breakfast in you, and be in court with plenty of time."

I stood up. "Well, thanks for everything, Sergeant."

"Not at all, sir."

"Where's the best place to catch a taxi?"

"Out to the street, then right to the next corner. Should be one along directly."

I nodded a good-bye of sorts, went through the entrance of the stationhouse, and out into what seemed to be a kind of alley or mews. I walked to the street without looking back, turned right, and headed for the corner. About halfway there, I spotted a dustbin, unpinned my carnation, and dropped it in. It had served its purpose. Somebody had recognized me all right.

Chapter
Three

*O*nly two days prior to spending that night in a London jail cell, Julia Child and I had been pounding hell out of a couple of boned chicken breasts when Myron Greene, my lawyer, the new millionaire, knocked on the door of my "deluxe" efficiency on the ninth floor of the Adelphi on East Forty-sixth. There was an ivory-colored doorbell that Myron Greene could have pressed, but he knew better because it didn't work, and hadn't worked in three years. The Adelphi Apartment-Hotel was that kind of a place.

I put my stainless-steel mallet down on the ancient butcher block that I had recently acquired from a seventy-two-year-old Brooklyn butcher who had said to hell with it and gone out of business the day that prime porterhouse hit $4.25 a pound. I nodded as Julia Child dipped the pounded chicken breasts, first into the nutmeg-seasoned flour, and then into the lightly beaten egg yolk. "I got it, Julia," I said, switched off the television set, and went to the door.

Myron Greene stood there for a moment, eyeing me with the same faint disapproval that he probably eyed all grown men who answer their doors at four in the afternoon dressed only in terry-cloth bathrobe and denim apron.

"Jesus Christ," he said.

"Not bad; how are you?"

He came in and looked around the way that he always did, as though expecting to find a badly mismanaged seraglio. While he looked, I took the opportunity to examine what a bright New York attorney, who had just become a millionaire at thirty-eight, might wear on a nice warm May day.

If he had been born about a century and a half earlier, Myron Greene probably would have been a disciple of Beau Brummell, a slightly plump disciple perhaps, but nevertheless a devoted one. As it was, he contented himself with dressing about six months behind the latest cry which, on that particular May afternoon, happened to be a half-hearted revival of the zoot suits of the wartime forties.

Myron Greene was wearing a modified version of one, a powder blue number with a jacket that draped almost to his knees. High-waisted britches went halfway up his chest and were held there by two-inch-wide midnight blue suspenders. His brown, graying hair, still modishly long, glistened with what I suspected of being a pound or two of Vaseline.

"My, you're pretty," I said.

"Like it?" he said in a half-serious, half-hopeful tone.

"What happened to the key chain?" I said. "You know, those three- or four-foot-long jobs that they used to wear?"

Myron Greene glanced down. "I thought it might be just a bit much."

"Maybe," I said. "Well, congratulations anyhow."

"On what?"

"On the Centennial Group. I heard that it hit one twenty-one at two o'clock yesterday afternoon so that

14

makes you a millionaire, if you exercised your options which, knowing you, you sure as hell did."

Myron Greene shrugged at my news about the stock of the conglomerate that he had helped put together nearly six months ago. "It's all on paper," he said.

"Well, it must be fun to tot up the figures anyway."

He shrugged again, his eyes still wandering around the apartment. "That's new," he said, indicating the butcher block that stood before the Pullman kitchen.

"Actually, it's a hundred and nineteen years old."

"Where'd you get it?"

"Brooklyn."

"How much?"

"Fifty bucks—and another fifty to get it hauled up here."

"It's still a good investment."

"Jesus, Myron, I didn't buy it as an investment."

"Maybe you should've."

"Let's have a drink first."

"First before what?"

"Before the bad news that dragged you out of your office at four o'clock on the afternoon that you became a millionaire."

Myron Greene looked at his watch. "I'm thirty-eight."

"Is that what your watch says?"

Myron Greene sighed and sat down in one of the chairs around the hexagonal poker table. "If it had happened when I was twenty-eight, it might have meant something. I don't know what though."

"Here," I said, setting a Scotch and water down in front of him. "It's got the meaning of life in it."

Myron Greene took a swallow of the drink and then looked slowly around the room. "At least you've lived," he said.

It was really the reason that I was Myron Greene's client. He was convinced that I led a spicy existence peopled with long-legged blondes, likeable adventurers, and fairly honest crooks and thieves, all of whom had hearts of gold. I was, in Myron Greene's eyes, a tear-around with an enviable life-style designed almost exclusively for fun and frolic, but highlighted here and there with the occasional thrill of mild danger.

In reality, I was turning into a recluse who spent too much time alone in museums, galleries, motion pictures, and at any parade that happened to come along. I also drank too much in bars in the company of minor thieves, con men, prospering cops, failed gamblers, fast-buck hustlers, and others of their ilk such as out-of-work actors and free-lance writers.

In my spare time, of which there was virtually no end, I stayed home, stared at the walls, looked at too much television, and read too much Dickens and Camus. On most Saturdays I got to see my eight-year-old son whose mother had married a man who, unlike Myron Greene, had made his first million at twenty-three. He was thirty-five now and apparently well on the way to his first billion.

My son was never really quite sure what it was that I did for a living. "You mean you get things back for people, Dad?"

"That's right."

"You mean if somebody lost something, like a whole lot of money, you'd help them find it?"

"No, I help people get things back that they've had stolen from them. It's never money."

"What things?"

"Well, jewelry, for instance. Or personal papers. Or valuable art such as paintings and pictures and things. Sometimes, even people."

"You mean people get stolen?"

"Sometimes."

"And you go find them and then arrest the crooks?"

"No, I go and buy the people or the things back."

He had to think about that for a moment. "And the people who have things stolen, they pay you to go buy them back from the crooks, huh?"

"Sometimes," I said. "Sometimes the crooks pay me."

"How much?" he said. I could see that his stepfather was teaching him a thing or two.

"Ten percent," I said. "Suppose you had something stolen."

"My bicycle."

"All right, your bicycle. And suppose whoever stole it was willing to sell it back to you for ten dollars."

"It's worth more than that. A lot more."

"I know. So the crooks would say that if you'd use me to bring the money to them, they'd let you have the bike back for ten dollars."

He had to think about that, too. "I guess so," he said finally. "But how do I know that they wouldn't just take the ten dollars and keep my bike?" He was also growing up a true New Yorker.

"Because I wouldn't let them. No bike, no money."

"And how much would you charge me?"

"I wouldn't charge you anything. But if it were somebody else, some boy I didn't know, I'd charge him a dollar."

"And he'd have to pay that?"

"Either he or the crook who stole the bike."

"Huh," my son said. "That's a funny business."

"You're right."

"What do you call it? I mean, what do you call what you do?"

"I'm a go-between," I said, feeling a little foolish.

He shook his head slowly. "I never heard of that before."

"There're not too many of us around."

"Mama always says you're a writer."

"Not anymore."

"She says you used to work on a newspaper."

"That was a long time ago. The paper went out of business."

"When?"

"About the time you were born."

17

"Did you write about football?"

"No, I wrote a column."

"About what?"

"People."

"What kind of people?"

"All kinds. I wrote about crooks a lot."

"And who else?"

"Oh, funny people. People who do funny things for a living."

"Like you do now?"

"Uh-huh. Like I do now."

"Do you do this every day?" he said. "I mean do you go buy things back every day for people who've had them stolen from them?"

"Not every day."

"When do you do it?"

"Oh, about once or twice a year. Sometimes three times."

"Do you make a lot of money?"

"No. Not a lot."

"Do you make as much as Jack?" Jack was his new father.

"Nobody makes as much as Jack."

"Do you make as much as Uncle Myron?"

"Not quite."

"I bet you make as much as Eddie."

This time I had to think. Eddie was the bell captain at the Adelphi, and a special pal of my son's. Eddie was not only a bell captain, he was also a slum landlord, the owner of a taxicab fleet consisting of two cabs, a minor bookmaker, and—when pressed—a reliable procurer. "Well, Eddie might make just a little more than I do."

"Are you poor, Dad?"

"You'll have to ask your uncle Myron about that," I said.

"You're broke, you know," Myron Greene said after taking another swallow of his drink.

18

"I'm not surprised," I said. "It's about time."

"Well, you're not really broke. You've got a few thousand left."

When he wasn't putting conglomerates together, or finding fairly legal ways for his enormously rich clients to become even richer, Myron Greene gave some attention to my affairs, such as they were. He saw to it that my bills were paid; touted me on stocks that I never bought (invariably to my regret); kept me even, or just a little ahead, with the Internal Revenue Service, and insisted that I squirrel some away each year in a Keogh plan for my golden retirement years which, as far as I could tell, had already arrived.

And it was to Myron Greene that the rich and their insurance companies came when they wanted to ransom something that had been stolen from them, usually something which they were rather fond of, or at least accustomed to having around—a diamond necklace, a Klee, or perhaps a nine-year-old daughter.

Or sometimes it was the thieves themselves who made the initial contact with Myron Greene. He liked to talk to them. In fact, he liked to talk to them so much that they sometimes couldn't get him off the phone and I later had to explain that among other things, Myron Greene would like to have been a flashy criminal lawyer, if there had been any real money in it.

So it was through Myron Greene that the go-between assignments came to me, usually two, sometimes three a year, and for his services he got ten percent of my ten percent and whatever pleasure it was that he found in skirting the world of the thief.

Now as he sat at my poker table brooding about having become a millionaire ten years too late for it to mean anything, I said, "Well, there must be some alternative to welfare."

Myron Greene sighed, "You're getting up there, too, you know."

"I'm six months older than you are."

"Middle-aged," he said.

"I don't feel middle-aged, but then I get a lot of rest."

"You have real talent," he said. "Have you ever thought of putting it to work again?"

"You mean a steady job?"

Myron Greene nodded.

"I dreamt about it last Friday, I think it was, but before it got really bad, I woke up."

Myron Greene sighed again. "Well, I got a call earlier this afternoon. Long distance."

"From where?"

"London," he said. "London, England."

"I thought that that's where London was."

"It involves a goodly sum."

"How much?"

"One hundred thousand."

"That's not bad."

"Pounds."

"That's even better. Who called?"

"He said he was a friend of yours. Or at least a close acquaintance."

"Who?"

"A Mr. Apex."

"English Eddie," I said.

"Yes," Myron Greene said, "he did say his name was Edward. He also sounded awfully British."

"He's not," I said.

"What is he?"

"He's American. He was reared in Detroit and his real name's Eddie Apanasewicz and when I knew him he was probably the best international con man around."

Chapter
Four

Before the second world war, English Eddie Apex's widowed mother had taught various sons and daughters of the Polish aristocracy in Warsaw how to speak the King's English. It was more the Queen's English really, the upper class English of Victoria's time, with virtually no contractions, beautifully savored vowels, and consonants that were bitten off at the quick. And if it sounded slightly stilted, it had a wonderfully redeeming lilt to it, the legacy of the wandering Welsh scholar-linguist who had settled in Warsaw after the first world war and from whom Eddie Apex's mother had learned her perfect English, along with her equally perfect French and German. I was once told that, even years later, exiled Poles could always tell which of their number had studied with Madame Apanasewicz.

In the late summer of 1939, she accepted the aid of some of her former students and left Poland for London. She took with her only her last remaining student, who was her nine-year-old son Edward, and who had been named, for girlishly romantic notions, after the Prince of Wales, later Edward VIII, and even later, the Duke of Windsor.

She stayed in London only a week or two and then sailed for Canada where she arrived just as war broke out in Europe. With the help of distant relatives, she and her son emigrated from Canada to Detroit, where they both became naturalized American citizens in 1945.

Meanwhile, her nine-year-old son, dressed in his old European clothes and speaking English like Freddie Bartholomew, only better, had the opportunity of going to grade school in Detroit with the sons and daughters of the workers who assembled automobiles, and later, during the war, tanks and airplanes.

If he had been a delicate child, Eddie Apex's story probably would be different. But he was a big-boned boy, large for his age, with oversized hands that he quickly learned to form into oversized fists. "The ones that I really had trouble with were the crackers, the southern kids," he later said. "They told me that I talked 'funny.' I couldn't even understand what they were saying for the first six months. All I knew was that I had to beat hell out of them before they beat hell out of me."

Eddie Apex's mother, after working in a department store for eight years, died in 1947, the year that her son managed to graduate from high school. At seventeen and a half, he looked nearer to twenty-one or twenty-two. He was six-foot-two of big-boned brawn, green-eyed and fair-haired, narrow-hipped and wide-shouldered, and looked, indeed, like nothing so much as an all-American college wingback who spoke in the tones of Mayfair rather than Michigan.

With nothing to keep him in Detroit, Eddie Apex headed for New York where he found his accent to be an asset rather than a liability, at least in the crowd that he fell in with, which in an earlier day might be said to have consisted solely of evil companions. They were for the most part veterans of World War Two who had discovered the rewards of the black markets in Europe and Asia and were then looking for enterprises that would prevent them from doing something distasteful, such as going to work.

"We came up with the Lost English Cousin Con," Eddie Apex told me years later. "One of my chaps had a couple of years of law school and he had a girl friend who worked for this fey genealogist who made a pretty good living by coming up with phony family trees for people who wanted to claim kin with British aristocracy. Well, that was our sucker list. My job was to pose as the mark's long-lost cousin, fresh off the boat from London, who was in the states looking for a relative who could save the family castle. Well, to make a long story short, we made it appear to the mark that he could beat me out of a million-dollar estate for a mere twenty-five or fifty thousand dollars. Greed won. It always does, of course, and the mark wound up owning some awfully fancy parchment documents—all carefully aged, of course."

From that time on until 1963, English Eddie Apex, the surname he legally adopted on his twenty-first birthday, worked his various scams in most of the world's playgrounds from Acapulco to the Aegean, earning himself a reputation among the cognoscenti as probably "the best long con man in the business."

I became privy to all these trade tricks in 1963 when English Eddie came to New York to announce his retirement at the age of thirty-three. He had never been arrested and he had never spent a minute in jail, but he was finding it more and more difficult to travel without spending hours on end in the company of immigration officials, none of whom was particularly anxious to have him set up shop within their particular borders.

"Christ," he said, "I can scarcely get into Switzerland anymore. When you can't get in there with a bagful of money, you know things are bad."

So English Eddie Apex decided to retire and to announce his retirement through my column, if I were willing, which I was. I spent nearly a week with him and got two good columns out of it and one visit from a fraud squad detective who wanted to know if I really thought that English Eddie was hanging up his gloves.

"I think so," I said. "He's made enough."

The detective nodded. "Like he says, he's rich now."

"That's right."

"Yeah, well, that's what I mean. It's like he also says in your column, the rich always want to get more."

"Maybe," I said, "but maybe he'll go legit."

The detective nodded again, gloomily. "Yeah, and my cat'll whistle 'Stardust,' too."

The day after my last column on Eddie Apex appeared, he dropped by my office and handed me a carefully wrapped box. I opened it while he watched. It was an alligator wallet, obviously expensive. "I would have offered you money, but I didn't think you'd take it," he said, sounding to me for all the world like Richard Burton imitating a terribly bored captain of the guards.

"You're right," I said. "I wouldn't."

"It's rather a good wallet," he said. "It should last you for years."

"Well, thanks very much."

"It's nothing really. Oh, by the way, I think I told you that I was retiring to Mexico?"

"That's what you told me."

"Well, just let it stand that way. But actually I'm not."

"Not retiring?"

"Oh, I'm retiring right enough, but not to Mexico."

"Where then?"

"London."

"Why London?"

"Well, it's obvious, isn't it?"

"What?"

He grinned his charming, con man's grin. "I can pass there."

When he was gone, I examined the wallet. It had one of these semi-secret compartments and when I looked into it I found five one-hundred-dollar bills. I took them down to a bank to see whether they were any good and when I found that they were, I went out and bought something for my wife that was ridiculously expensive, but for the life of me I can't remember what it was.

"What did he want?" I asked, after telling a fascinated Myron Greene a lot of what I knew about English Eddie Apex.

"He was rather vague until we got down to the question of money."

"He usually perks up there."

"He said that he was calling me instead of you because he'd heard that I represented you, which he thought was sound because when it comes to negotiating in your own behalf, he didn't think you'd be too effective."

"I don't have your drive, Myron."

Myron Greene nodded his agreement at that. "Well, it seems that a work of art has been stolen from a party or parties that Mr. Apex is representing. The thieves are willing to sell it back for one hundred thousand pounds. The owner—or owners, I'm not sure which because Apex would sometimes say 'they' and sometimes 'he' when referring to whomever it was stolen from—anyway, they or he are willing to engage your services as go-between for the usual ten percent. At this point, of course, we started negotiating. I asked for your expenses. Mr. Apex declined, but countered with an offer of earnest money— ten percent of your fee to be deposited in your bank here. I told him that I thought fifteen percent of your fee in advance would be far more in line in view of the fact that you would be paying your own expenses. We settled for twelve and a half percent in advance. I must say that Apex seems quite good at doing large sums in his head."

"He didn't say what had been stolen?" I said.
"No."
"Or from whom?"

"No."

"It's probably hot then."

"Really? What makes you think so?" It was obvious that Myron Greene would be delighted if it were. Shady dealings always fascinated him.

"Let's look at it this way," I said. "Firstly, Eddie Apex is involved. I don't think I need a secondly."

"You said he retired."

"He retired from the con, not from crime."

"He certainly sounds straightforward," Myron Greene said.

"He hasn't lost his touch then. You notice he didn't say what was stolen or from whom. You know as well as I do, Myron, that when any valuable art is stolen, the first to be notified is the insurance company and the second is the police. And usually it's the insurance company or another lawyer who calls you. Or maybe the thieves themselves. But here we've got an ex-con artist calling on behalf of clients unnamed about an unmentionable work of art that somebody has stolen and is willing to sell back for nearly a quarter of a million dollars. That means that its true market value must be close to a million or more. But no insurance company seems to be involved. No lawyer. And certainly no police. That makes it sound hot to me."

"Possibly," Myron Greene said. "You present a good case. However, it may be that whatever was stolen was uninsurable—or even that whoever stole it threatened to destroy it, if the police were brought in. We've known cases like that before."

"Kidnappings mostly."

We sat there at the poker table in silence for a while until I got up and mixed us both another drink. "I perhaps neglected to mention that the earnest money that Apex agreed to advance is nonreturnable," he said.

My admiration for Myron Greene's ability as a skilled negotiator rose several more degrees. "You talked *Eddie Apex* out of that?"

Myron Greene smiled for perhaps the first time that day, the day that he became a millionaire. "He did take a bit of convincing," he said as modestly as he could. "Of course, it means that you'll have to go to London to find out what the deal is. If you don't like it, you can turn it down and, except for your expenses, you'll have made twelve hundred and fifty pounds or approximately three thousand dollars."

"Apex won't talk about it over the phone?"

"No."

"Why doesn't he just write us a letter?"

Myron Greene smoothed his hair. "There's a time factor."

"What time factor?"

"You have to be there tomorrow night."

We shared another silence and after a few moments I said, "Well, London should be pleasant this time of year."

"You lived there once, didn't you?"

"Uh-huh. A long time ago for about a year. It was when the paper thought that I might do the same thing for London that Buchwald was doing for Paris. It didn't work out though."

"What happened?"

"I got homesick."

Chapter
Five

At ten minutes to nine on the morning after the night that I had lodged in jail, I was sitting on a bench in a long brown and green hall just off the Marlborough Street Magistrates courtroom, sharing out my cigarettes with about thirty or so other bums, layabouts, wifebeaters, and meth drinkers. Metropolitan police flowed up and down the hall, stopping now and again to exchange a friendly word or two with what seemed to be some fairly regular customers.

I was shaved, showered, breakfasted, and suited up in a glen plaid number with a black knit tie that I hoped would make me look respectable and even, with luck, a bit stuffy. I sat there on the bench, half-listening to a tall, thin Australian, bony as a sackful of antlers, counsel me that if I really wanted to do some serious drinking, I should drop down around Earls Court where the pommy bastards would leave you alone, at least most of the time.

I was nodding away at this when a police constable stopped in front of me. He had blond hair, sideburns, and pale blue eyes that were still no friendlier than they had been the evening before in front of the Black Thistle.

"Well, Mr. St. Ives, you're looking a bit better this morning."

I nodded. "Constable Wilson, isn't it?"

"That's right, sir. I must say you were coming on a bit strong yesterday, what with your karate chops and all."

"I don't know any karate chops," I said. "I thought I was being mugged."

"In broad daylight?" Constable Wilson seemed almost shocked at the idea.

"Sorry," I said, "I keep forgetting that it can't happen here."

"Well, certainly not can't, but when it does, it's usually the coloreds involved."

"Why a night in the pokey and a day in court?" I said. "Why didn't you just pour me in a taxi and ship me home?"

"Huh," he said. "Put you in the hands of that lot in your condition and you would've been mugged. Or worse."

"I thought all London taxi drivers were polite. Friendly."

He grinned, but I couldn't detect much humor in it. "Like all London bobbies, right?"

"Sure."

"Well, we might have done, if you hadn't come on with that karate."

"I don't know any karate," I said.

Finally, my name was called and I was in the courtroom, standing in the dock, feeling something like a latterday Jack the Ripper, and there was Constable Wilson presenting his case, telling everybody how drunk I had been, but that I didn't have any previous record, and the magistrate, not really caring, asked me how I chose to plead, and after I said that I chose to plead guilty, I was told to step down and pay the man.

The man was back down the long hall and up a flight of stairs that led to the Chief Clerk's office where a friendly looking type who was about forty pounds overweight kept up a steady line of chatter with what, for the most part, seemed to be an old and valued clientele.

When he got to me, I said, "St. Ives, Philip," and he ran his finger down a list and said, "Yes, sir, Mr. St. Ives. That'll be fifty pence, no checks accepted, and we hope everything has been satisfactory."

"It's been perfect," I said and handed him a pound. He gave me the change, a receipt, and a "Thank you very much, come again."

It was ten o'clock by the time I came out on to Marlborough and the gray Rolls was waiting right where it was supposed to be. The uniformed chauffeur held the door for me, I got in, and Eddie Apex said, "How did it go?"

"I was fined about a dollar twenty. I guess there's something to British justice after all."

"You'd better tell me about it again," he said.

"I've already told you about it."

"You sounded groggy when I talked to you this morning."

"Has this thing got a bar?" I said.

"Of course. Whisky?"

"Whisky's fine."

It was a fitted bar with cut-glass bottles and crystal tumblers. Eddie Apex poured me a drink, but didn't fix one for himself. "Still a bit early for me."

"By jet lag it's four in the afternoon," I said and took a sip of the drink. It was good Scotch, possibly the best, but with my cigarette palate, I couldn't be sure.

"All right," he said, "let's go over it again."

I looked out the window. We were on Edgware Road and turning west into Bayswater Road at Marble Arch.

"We'll go to my place," he said.

"Okay. I'll run it by again. I got into Heathrow on Pan Am at around nine yesterday morning. I caught a cab and went to the Hilton. I called you and told you I'd arrived and we agreed to meet at eight that evening. After that, I ordered up breakfast and a couple of drinks and then

I went to bed. At four o'clock my phone rang. It was a man. He didn't try to disguise his voice. He said that he represented the people that you were dealing with and since they were now going to be dealing with me, they'd like to look me over. I said fine. They told me to buy a carnation, wear it in my lapel, and be at the Black Thistle on New Cavendish Street at six-fifteen sharp. I called you, but the guy who answered your phone said you were out and wouldn't be back until seven. Well, the Hilton didn't have a red carnation, so I bought a pink one and arrived at the pub about ten minutes early. I bought a drink, but before I could take a swallow, a rather tweedy type knocked it out of my hand with his elbow."

"What did he look like?" Apex said. "The tweedy type."

"Late twenties, running to fat, about six feet tall, bald and blond, pinkfaced, with a two-inch scar on his crown. The scar was puckered. Mean anything to you?"

"Nothing."

"Well, he insisted on buying me another drink. I agreed and that was my mistake. He doped the drink. I know that there's nothing that's supposed to work that fast, but it did."

"Chloral hydrate won't work like that," Apex said.

"It wasn't chloral hydrate. Chloral hydrate just makes you go to sleep. This stuff caused awful cramps, then nausea, and then euphoria."

"Then you got into the fight with the coppers."

"That's right—and spent the night in jail."

"What do you think?" Apex said.

"What do I think? For Christ's sake, Eddie, it's your territory. What do you think?"

"I've never been in on one like this before. That's why I asked what you think."

I finished my drink. "You haven't told me anything yet. You haven't told me what's been stolen or from whom. In fact, you haven't told me anything at all except welcome to London."

"We really haven't had a chance to talk, have we?"

"No. We haven't."

"So what do you think?"

"About last night?"

"Yes."

"Well, I think you're dealing with some people who don't quite trust you," I said.

Apex nodded. "I already know that."

"And they wanted to find out whether they could trust me. So they tell me to be at a certain pub at a certain time, drug my drink, and watch me get arrested."

"Do you think the cops were in on it?"

"Not in on it, but they would have been involved sooner or later. I would have passed out in the gutter if they hadn't come along when they did. And that must have been the object of it all—to get me arrested."

"Sort of a test, right?"

"I can't think of anything else. If I'd kicked up a fuss and started talking about drugged drinks and why I'm here and demanding to see the ambassador, the thieves would probably tell you to find yourself another go-between. But since I took it and kept my mouth shut, they'll probably figure that we can do business."

"Have you ever been through one like this before?" Apex said.

"No, but I've dealt with a lot of nervous types who've wanted to run a check on me. Usually it's meant nothing more than standing around some phone booth in a busy supermarket parking lot waiting for a call that never came. A lot of thieves, the amateurs especially, like to look the go-between over."

"What do you think of these, from what you've seen so far?" Apex said.

"I don't know what they've stolen yet, do I?"

"No, but what do you think? About the thieves, I mean."

"Well, they don't trust you, do they, Eddie?"

"No, they don't."

"Then I don't think they're amateurs."

33

Chapter Six

*T*he gray Rolls drew up in front of a four-story townhouse which was painted that peculiar thick London cream that can mask a lot of age as well as a lot of decay. We were in Knightsbridge and the house faced one of those well-cared-for little green squares that have a fence around them with locked gates to keep out the riffraff.

It was an expensive neighborhood, not too far from Harrods and even closer to Beauchamp Place where all the trendy shops were, and the Rolls looked right at home and, for that matter, so did English Eddie Apex.

He had aged well during the ten or eleven years since I had last seen him. He was a bit thicker around the middle, but the genius who had tailored his suit out of tiny gray worsted herringbones made you forget about the waist and concentrate on the marvelous thing that had been done for the shoulders. Apex wore a blue striped shirt with a white collar and cuffs and what could only have been a club tie because it was such a tatty blue and black. I estimated that he was wearing close to £150 on his back and maybe another £40 on his feet in the form of a pair of black loafers that shone like waxed marble.

He wasn't wearing a hat, and I could understand why. It might have mussed his hair which had been a deep, shining yellow when I had last seen him, the color of old gold—or perhaps new brass, since it belonged to Eddie Apex. Now it was a softly shining gray, the same shade as old, well-cared-for silver. Or new pewter.

Worn just long enough to be fashionable, his hair was almost the only thing about Apex that had changed. He was a little heavier, but not much, and there might have been a new line or two in his face, which was still as open as church and as honest as truth. Now in his early forties, Eddie Apex looked both distinguished and important enough to be a cabinet member, or a seasoned diplomat, or at least somebody who might be trusted to read the evening news over BBC. For some reason I found myself hoping very hard that Eddie Apex was still retired.

With the aid of the chauffeur, who looked almost old enough to be my grandfather, we got out of the Rolls, walked up a short curving flight of iron steps, through what may have been an Adams door, and into the center hall that was furnished with some stiff chairs and useless tables that looked uncomfortable and rickety enough to be antiques, although a lot of English furniture looks that way to me.

The elderly chauffeur had relinquished his care of us at the car and a stooped, thin man who might have been his uncle took over in the hall. He murmured, "Good morning, sir," to Apex, and ran his filmy blue eyes over me with what seemed to be disapproval, or perhaps disappointment over my not having anything to hand him such as a hat and cane.

"Jack, would you tell my wife that we'll be in the drawing room," Apex said, just as if he had been saying it all his life.

"Yes, sir," said Jack, the butler, and moved away with a surprisingly spry step for a man whose age I estimated to be around 102.

"You have any trouble with all this kid help of yours?" I said.

"They came with my wife," Apex said, opening a door for me.

"When did you get married?"

"About six years ago."

"That's about the time I got divorced," I said.

The drawing room was better than the center hall, in my opinion. It was modern, if you still happen to think that 1937 was modern. It was an oblong room, not quite narrow, and held an overabundance of chunky angular furniture heavily upholstered in some rather garish shades such as caution orange, schoolbus yellow, and roadmap green. There was a dark brown carpet on the floor and on the walls some flaming abstract paintings that I didn't much like either. Tucked away in the fireplace was that peculiar British invention, an electric space heater, which on a cold day might bring the room up to a cozy forty-seven degrees.

"Would you like something?" Apex said.

"What, for instance?"

"Another drink?"

"No, I don't think so."

"Tea?"

"Tea would be fine."

Apex moved over to the fireplace and pushed a button in a wall speaker that looked as if it had been recently installed—around 1951. "We would like some tea, please, Jack."

The box squawked something tinny that sounded very much like "Right away, sir."

I sat down in an orange chair with wide arms and Apex chose a yellow one. "Well," he said, "it's been a long time."

37

I looked around the room. "You're a long way from Cadillac Square."

"Yes, I am, aren't I."

"You like it here, I take it."

Apex nodded. "It's civilized."

"That's what they used to say about the Choctaws, until they got them riled or drunk or both."

"You don't find it so? Civilized, I mean?"

"I don't think London is any more civilized than any other big city. In many ways London is just like New York. They're both falling apart at the same places and if you're poor, they're both rotten places to live. If you're rich—well, if you're rich, almost anywhere is a good place to live."

"Strange you should say that," Apex said. "Most Americans like London."

"That's because a quaint brand of English is spoken here. If they spoke French here, you wouldn't get five tourists a year."

Eddie Apex smiled. "You exaggerate."

"Not much," I said. "Think it over while you're deciding when you're going to tell me why you got me over here."

"We brought you over here, Mr. St. Ives, to get our sword back." It was a drawling, husky voice and it came from behind me and it belonged to a woman. I rose and turned. She was standing in the doorway of the drawing room, smiling a little, and gazing at me with eyes that reminded me of a cat's, the half-wild kind that hasn't lived around the hearth too long. But it was her high cheekbones and her artful makeup that probably caused her eyes to look that way, that and the fact that, like a cat, she didn't seem to blink very often.

Apex had risen and was smiling. "You haven't met Ceil, have you?"

"No," I said. "I haven't. Hello, Mrs. Apex."

She crossed the room and held out her hand, still

smiling. "I hope, Mr. St. Ives, that you won't be disappointed to learn that I adore listening at keyholes."

"Nothing I like better myself," I said, "unless it's reading other people's mail."

"Oh, do you like to do that, too?"

"I also have a few other failings."

She let go of my hand and cocked her head to one side, studying me with those eyes that I saw were somewhere between blue and green. "And you're going to be our go-between. How nice."

"I'm going to discuss it, at least."

Before she could say anything else, Jack, the ancient butler, wheeled in the tea trolley.

"Oh, good, tea," she said. "Over here, Jack, I think." Over here was near a straight-backed chair that had been covered with a green material that I thought might have looked better on a snooker table. She lowered herself into the chair and then waited for the old man to roll the tea trolley over.

"Thank you, Jack," she said.

"Will the gentleman be staying for luncheon, mum?"

"Didn't I tell you? We'll all be going to Father's for lunch."

"I'll tell cook then, mum. She won't like it, will she? But I'll tell her."

"And I'll tell Father hello for you. And Uncle Norbert, too."

"Yes, mum. You do that. Tell him I said hello. And your uncle, too. Him, too. And I'll tell cook that there'll be nobody for lunch. Nobody at all." The old man stood there for a moment as if trying to think of somebody else he should tell, and when he couldn't, he turned and moved briskly away with his spry step.

"Poor old Jack," Ceil Apex said.

"How old is he?"

"Jack? I don't really know."

"He was a wedding gift," Apex said.

"He wasn't either," she said. "It was just that when Dad and Uncle Norbert moved into their new flat, there wasn't room for Jack. Or Tom either."

"Tom's the chauffeur," Apex said. "He was a wedding gift, too."

"Of course, Tom's younger than Jack," Ceil Apex said. "At least ten years younger."

"Tom's only seventy," Apex said.

"Jack's not eighty."

"How old was Jack when you first remember him?"

She thought about it as she arranged the teacups. "Well, he was getting on even then and that was twenty years ago—when I first remember him."

More like twenty-five years ago, I thought, as I sat there watching her pour the tea. I guessed her age at being around thirty, a year either way. She had one of those faces in which the bones are just right and she would look the same at forty as she did now and not much older at fifty unless her neck and throat started to go. Her hair was that light ash blond color that she could start frosting at thirty-five or so and nobody would ever know whether it was really going gray or not. Although her cat eyes were her best feature, she had a nice nose and a firm chin, perhaps a little too firm, and one of those wide, happy-looking mouths that seldom seemed to be still, even if she weren't talking. She wasn't a beauty, at least not in the accepted meaning of the word, but she had a face that would stay with you for a long time.

"How do you like your tea, Mr. St. Ives?" she said.

"With a little sugar."

Apex was still up so I sat there and let him hand me my cup and then we were all sitting there, sipping our tea and smiling at each other in the big house in Knightsbridge and except for our clothes, it might have been May of 1938.

"You mentioned a sword," I said.

"Yes, I did, didn't I?" she said.

"Do you know much about swords, Phil?" Apex said.

"Next to nothing. I know even less about any sword that's worth one hundred thousand pounds. Unless it's Excalibur."

"Or Durandel," Ceil said and smiled.

"Roland's, right?"

"See," she said to her husband. "He does know something about them."

"Look at his face," he said.

She studied it for a moment. "Apprehension mingled with skepticism, I'd say."

Apex nodded. "He thinks I've come out of retirement." He grinned at me. "Ceil knows all about what I once did to make ends meet."

"He was very good at it, too, did you know that, Mr. St. Ives?"

"So I've heard," I said. "But it doesn't sound like him."

"What?"

"King Arthur's sword would be a little gamey even for you, wouldn't it, Eddie?"

This time he laughed. "I might have worked it for five hundred quid now and again, but not for a hundred thousand."

"But there is a sword?" I said.

Apex nodded.

"And it's been stolen?"

"From my father," Ceil Apex said. "And uncle."

"And the thieves want a hundred thousand pounds to hand it back?"

"That's right."

"So it's worth how much?"

Apex thought about it. "At a million pounds, it would be a steal; at two million pounds, an irresistible bargain."

"It's hot then, isn't it?" I said. "I mean there wouldn't be all this hush-hush about it, if it weren't hot."

Apex glanced at his wife. They smiled at each other.

"Well, I suppose you could say it's hot, but the rightful owner's not going to do much complaining."

"Why?"

"Because," Apex said, "he's been dead for about eight hundred years."

Chapter
Seven

Ceil Apex's father and uncle lived in a mansion. Although not a term to be used indiscriminately, the four-story, dark stone building took up nearly a third of a block on Groom Place, virtually within hailing distance of Belgrave Square. Of course, Groom Place is a short street and from its name, I assumed that it may not have been too fashionable at one time, perhaps a few centuries back, but to me the big stone house was still a mansion and I suspected that it was to most people who are at all interested in the opulent.

Neither Eddie Apex nor his wife had been willing to tell me anything more about the sword that was supposed to be an irresistible bargain at two million pounds. They had insisted that I wait until lunch so that I could hear it from the two men it had been stolen from.

"This is what you call a flat?" I said to Ceil Apex as we got out of the Rolls with old Tom's help and walked up a short flight of stone steps.

"Oh, they don't have the entire place," she said. "They have only the first two floors. Some big-rich Greek has the other two, but he's seldom there. There're separate entrances, of course."

"I was worried about that."

She laughed. "After Eddie and I were married it gave Father and Uncle Norbert an excuse to splurge a bit. I'm afraid they might have overdone it."

From the outside the building was nothing spectacular, just a big, square, four-storied structure with a flat roof. It was built out of a dark red, almost purplish stone and architecturally I thought it was a bust. But someday, I kept telling myself, I was going to move out of my "deluxe" efficiency in the Adelphi and into some place decent and even perhaps a bit posh. So I kept up with real estate trends in some of the world's high rent districts, places such as New York's upper East Side, Paris, Rome, St. Thomas, and Aspen, Colorado. I also, more out of horrified curiosity than real interest, kept abreast of rents and land values in London's West End, at least in its more fashionable sections such as Mayfair, Belgravia, Chelsea, Knightsbridge, and Kensington. In my high cost of shelter race, London won going away, with New York in place and Paris in show. Rome was a close fourth and St. Thomas and Aspen tied for fifth. And I kept on renewing my lease at the Adelphi.

So I didn't even try to guess what it cost Ceil Apex's father and uncle to live where they did. I assumed only that they were extremely wealthy, perhaps even rich. After all, the rich were the only ones who could afford English Eddie Apex as a son-in-law.

There was no superannuated butler to open the door for us at the house on Groom Place. Instead, there was something young and curvy, dressed in a black dress that may have been a uniform, but whether it was or not, was at least three sizes too small, and perhaps three or four inches too short. She had a round olive face and dark eyes and a very white smile which she turned on at the sight of Ceil Apex. She also bobbed up and down in something that resembled a curtsey.

"Hello, Luisa," Ceil Apex said.

"Miss Ceil; welcome," the girl said, or something that sounded very much like that.

Ceil Apex turned to her husband. "Ask her where Father and Uncle Norbert are."

Apex started speaking to the girl in a language that I at first took to be Spanish, but which I finally decided was Portuguese. He would speak Portuguese, of course. At one time there had been some fat prospects in his line of work in Rio.

It was a brief, animated conversation with much giggling and eye-rolling on the part of Luisa and some expressive Latinate gestures from Apex who, I decided, plunged right into whatever role he played.

"What was that all about?" his wife said as we followed the maid down a long, wide hall.

"They're in the red room," Apex said.

"That wasn't all she said."

"I asked her if she were getting any."

"And she said she was, I trust."

"She said that life was very full." Apex looked at me. "Maybe you understand now why we're saddled with old Tom and Jack. Ceil's dad and uncle are a couple of aging goats. When they moved here they hired four of these Portuguese bints to look after them. The old boys run a regular harem."

"You're just jealous, darling," his wife said.

"You're right. I am."

At the end of the long wide hall that was lined with heavy oiled furniture and dim old paintings, the girl opened a door and stood to one side, smiling warmly at all of us. I thought that she probably smiled most of the time.

The red room was just that. Red. The walls were red plush and the curtains were red velvet and there was a dark maroon carpet on the floor and on it rested a lot of curved, ornate furniture that must have gone back to Victoria's time. All of the furniture, except for some massive oak and mahogany tables, seemed to be upholstered in various shades of blending reds. There were also some paintings that looked vaguely familiar and there was one above the mantel that I especially wanted to take a closer look at once the introductions were over.

"Mr. St. Ives," she said, "this is my father, Ned Nitry, and my uncle, Norbert Nitry."

I shook hands with Ned first and then with Norbert. Both of them had Ned's daughter's eyes, except that where hers were blue-green, theirs were a tawny brown, so I suppose it was their bone structure she had and not their eyes. And while she had the look about her of a half-wild cat, they had the look of a couple of lazy lions who were getting a little long in the tooth, but not so much so that they couldn't make their authority felt when they thought it was worth the effort.

"Do sit down, Mr. St. Ives, do," said Ned Nitry and I sat down in a low plush armchair with an oval back.

Norbert Nitry moved over to a drinks tray and said, "Well, what're we having, a touch of whisky? Whisky's your drink, Eddie. What about you, Mr. St. Ives?"

"Whisky's his drink, too, Bert," Apex said.

"Water or soda?"

"Water," I said.

"And sherry for my girl and gin and it for Ned and me," Norbert Nitry said, mixed the drinks deftly, and served them around.

We sat there in the mansion in Belgravia and tasted our drinks and the scene was fine but the accents were all wrong. At least, the Nitry brothers' accents were. They were both in their sixties, probably their early sixties, but it was hard to tell which was the elder. They were both of medium height and plump, if not fat, although it didn't show in their faces too much because of those bones. They were closely barbered faces, a healthy pink, and although their hair might have been thinning on top it was thick and gray and long above the ears. They resembled each other enough to be taken for brothers, but not for twins. Ceil Apex's father, Ned, had a mouth that was a bit thinner and a bit firmer than his brother's. A bit harder really. Despite the careful barbering and the tendency toward plumpness, there was nothing soft about either of those faces with their tired lion eyes, blunt noses, lump chins, and those tight, wide mouths that twenty years ago might have been tough. Or just mean.

And although their tailor, probably the same one patronized by Eddie Apex, had done wonders for their figures, nobody had done anything for their accents which to me sounded more like Lambeth than Belgravia. I'm not that good on English accents. I can distinguish between Manchester and Mayfair, but not between Oxford and Sandhurst, if, indeed, there is anything to distinguish. The people who had sat on those same red plush Victorian chairs seventy-five or eighty years ago would, without a qualm, have called the Nitry brothers' accents lower class. I'm not sure what they would have been called today. Working class maybe. Such accents in England were supposed to be a handicap to one's upward economic mobility although they didn't seem to have bothered the Nitry brothers any.

"Well," Ned Nitry said, "Eddie tells us that you've already done a job of work for us."

"I spent a night in jail, if that's what you mean."

"Doped your drink, did they?"

"That's right."

"I'm not surprised. They're probably a nasty lot."

"You're talking about the thieves."

"Correct. The thieves."

"What did they steal from you?"

"Didn't Eddie tell you?"

"He said they stole a sword. Offhand, I can't think of many swords that're worth anywhere near two or three million pounds."

"Well, Bert's our sword expert," he said, turning to Uncle Norbert. "Tell him about the sword, Bert."

Bert took a swallow of his gin, leaned his head back, and looked at the ceiling with the practiced gesture of the expert tale spinner. "Know much about the swords that were used in the age of chivalry, Mr. St. Ives?" he said, sounding the "ch" in chivalry like the "ch" in church.

"Your son-in-law exhausted my knowledge earlier today," I said. "I know about Excalibur and Roland's sword, Durandel, but the rest of what I know I got mostly from Prince Valiant."

"Valiant? I can't recall a Prince Valiant."

"He's in a comic strip but the guy who draws him seems to be fussy about details."

"Well, no matter," Bert said. "Arthur and Roland are long before the time I'm talking about. Long before. I'm talking about the time of the Crusades from about 1099 up to 1250. That's A.D. Anno Domini."

"There must have been a lot of swords around about that time," I said because he had paused in his tale as if waiting for some comment and it was all I could think of to say.

"Ah, and what swords!" Uncle Bert said, warming to his subject. "Proper swords, they were, some with three-foot blades and perfect balance and weighing no more'n two or three pounds and sharp as carving knives, sharper than today's, in fact, and just the thing for slicing through chain mail and armor plate."

I remembered a film that I had seen as a child. It had been about the Crusades, probably the first one in 1099, and there had been a confrontation between the English and the Saracens. I guess they were the Saracens. At any rate, the Englishman was showing off his sword. He took an iron bar, about an inch thick, and with a mighty blow of his sword, slashed through it. The Saracen, an oily type, I recall, smiled disdainfully and said something such as, "You will still lose, Englishman. Your swords are not

48

sharp enough." And with that he drew his own, a wickedly curved job, tossed up a silk scarf, and let it float down upon his upturned blade which sliced it neatly in two.

"Have you ever heard of the Sword of St. Louis, Mr. St. Ives?"

"No."

"Well, there are stories and stories about it. Some true, I'd say, but most not. But before he became a Saint, Louis was King of France, King Louis the Ninth. That's fact. And in 1250 he led his Crusade into Egypt. That's fact. And that same year he was defeated and captured by the Saracens at Mansourah. And that's fact. But what happened to his sword?"

"I don't know."

"Nobody does," Norbert said. "Not really, they don't. Some say he buried it. Some say he painted it black and gave it to one of his knights for safekeeping. Nobody is quite sure what the knight did with it, but most think he flogged it."

"To whom?"

"Nobody knows; probably another knight. But we don't hear anything else about it, not even rumor, for nearly a century. Then it supposedly turns up in 1368, still in Egypt, but this time in the Hall of Victories in the Alexandria arsenal. It might have been taken by the Mameluke Sultans from somebody fighting with the king of Cyprus, Peter of Lusignan, who was also king of Jerusalem, titular king anyhow. He got defeated trying to take Cairo in 1365."

"Then what?" I said.

"Then nothing. Not for another two centuries when it shows up in Constantinople in 1573. After that, there's a rumor about its being in Moscow in 1731. The dimensions are right anyhow. The blade's exactly thirty-four and a half inches long; the weight's right, three pounds, two ounces; the crosspiece is straight, but curved down

49

slightly at the ends; the hilt is solid metal painted black, and the pommel is about the size and shape of an oversized Brazil nut."

"How did they know it was the same sword?" I said.

"The blade was the finest steel that ever came out of Bordeaux," Uncle Norbert said. "There and Milan and Passau, and Cologne and Augsburg. That's where your good steel came from then. It was engraved with Latin, too, Cristus Vincit, Cristus Reinat, Cristus Inperat. That was the war cry of the Third Crusade. That was engraved on one side. On the other side was engraving in Arabic to show that it belonged to the Alexandria arsenal."

"You seem to have its history down cold," I said.

"That I do, lad. It's our business to. Well, there was a Frenchman in Moscow who somehow either recognized the sword for what it was or just took a liking to it. At least they say he was a Frenchman. It was there in a church and he stole it and headed back for Paris. He got as far as Cologne where he was murdered and nothing more was heard of the Sword of St. Louis until it turned up in a shop on Shaftesbury Avenue where it went for twelve and six to our client's old dad. In 1939, that was."

Luisa, the Portuguese maid, came in and said something that sounded like, "Luncheon is served, sir."

"Well, let's have at it before it gets cold," Ned Nitry said. "Bert can go on with it while we eat."

We started filing out of the red room and down the hall and into a formal dining room filled with heavy furniture that seemed to be just as Victorian as everything in the house. But before we left the red room I went over and took a good look at the painting that hung above the mantel. It was the portrait of a man with a Van Dyke beard who was dressed in the style of the late 1890s.

Ned Nitry waited for me. "Caught your eye, did it?"

"It's an Eakins or I'll eat it," I said.

"You'll eat it then, lad. Not too many Eakins in England, you know. That's a copy."

"If it's a copy, I'll eat it."

Ned Nitry smiled at me. "You've got a fair eye, don't you?"

"I had to handle an Eakins once," I said.

"You mean be a go-between to get one back?"

"That's right."

"How much did they want? The thieves, I mean." He seemed interested.

"Not enough really. Only fifty thousand dollars."

Ned Nitry nodded. "You're right," he said. "Not near enough."

Lunch was grilled lamb chops with too much fat on them; Brussels sprouts, which I hate; something that resembled paella, which I took to be the Portuguese contribution; thin red wine, and more of the tale of the Sword of St. Louis from Uncle Norbert who told it with his mouth full most of the time.

"Now, you might well ask how did the sword get from Cologne to a shop on Shaftesbury. And that we don't know. It may be that a member of the BEF brought it back in eighteen or nineteen, but we don't know that, do we?"

"No," I said, "I don't suppose we do."

"Well, the old dad of our client collected the odd sword now and again, but mostly sword canes and rapiers and épées and that lot. And before he could do more than clean up the Sword of St. Louis a bit he went off to war and got himself killed later at Tobruk. In Africa. So for nearly thirty years the Sword of St. Louis just lay about collecting dust. Well, our client was only two or three when his dad got himself killed and he didn't pay much attention to the sword collection until he came down from Oxford in sixty-one. Then he got a little interested and started collecting a few of his own, but it wasn't until about three months ago that he paid much attention to the Sword of St. Louis."

"He was a bit hard up, he was," Ned Nitry said.

"That's right," his brother said. "He's a gambling man,

sad to say, and he owed a little money and he thought that maybe the old sword might be worth a bob or two. Well, it was a mess, from what I understand. The blade was all black with scale, but it wasn't rusted because the scale somehow had helped preserve it. The crosspiece, the hilt, and the pommel were all black with scale or paint or both. Well, he worked on it careful-like, mostly on the blade until he got that in damn fine shape. Then he started in on the hilt and crosspiece. Well, the hilt turned out to be gold. Solid gold. And as you know, gold won't rust. The crosspiece was steel, of course, but stuck into each end were two round red stones about the size of peas. Rubies, they are, real rubies."

"They should be worth something, even if he couldn't prove it was a Sword of St. Louis," I said.

"Worth a bit," Uncle Norbert said. "Worth a bit. But finally, our lad got to the pommel. You know what the pommel is?"

"Yes," I said.

"It's that piece at the end of the hilt that keeps your hand from slipping off. Well, like I said, it was about the size of a big Brazil nut or a small egg and it was painted black. So he starts cleaning that off, working careful-like again, you know, and underneath the dirt and paint and enamel and God knows what all, what do you think he found?"

"I don't know."

"Rock crystal. The pommel was made out of rock crystal. Some of them were back then. Not many, but some. But then he takes another look and it's not rock crystal at all."

Uncle Norbert paused in his story and looked around, smiling because apparently he enjoyed the way he had told it.

"All right," I said, "if it wasn't rock crystal, what was it?"

He leaned across the table toward me, his mouth full of lamb. "A diamond as big as an egg, that's what it was.

A perfect, uncut diamond as big as an egg and weighing 146.34 metric carats, that's what it was that Louis had stuck on the end of his hilt and what do you think of that, Mr. St. Ives?"

"I think Eddie's right," I said. "I think it would be a real bargain at three million pounds."

Chapter Eight

*T*he Portuguese maid served the sweet, which turned out to be some kind of yellow pudding with dark things stuck in it. Raisins, probably. I chose to pass. The rest of them ate theirs and seemed to like it. When Ceil Apex asked if I would like coffee, I declined. There are some things that it is better not to risk in England.

After dessert they seemed to be waiting for me to say something so I said, "Why me?"

"Why you as go-between?" Ned Nitry said.

"That's right."

"That's a fair question."

"I've got a few more."

"I'd think so. Well, to be plain about it, Mr. St. Ives, you weren't our first choice. Eddie here was."

"They wouldn't go for it, though," Apex said.

"The thieves?"

"That's right," Apex said. "They seemed to be all too familiar with my past exploits."

"So we drew up a short list," Ned Nitry said, "and read

it to 'em over the phone. After a couple of hours they called back and said you'd do."

"How'd you know I was into the go-between thing, Eddie?"

He smiled. "I'd heard it around."

"You'll have to do better than that," I said.

"Okay. Remember that pearl necklace you handled a couple of years ago back in Chicago?"

"Yes."

"Well, that was a friend of mine, I suppose you could say. Or at least an acquaintance. He worked the states for a couple of years. When the insurance company called you in on the pearls, he was a little suspicious, so he checked you out. You've got an impressive reputation, my friend thinks. So when the thieves asked us about you, Ned told them to talk to this friend of mine. He must have given you a glowing report. He also told me that we should get in touch with you through your Mr. Greene, so I did."

"All right," I said. "When was it stolen?"

"Five days ago," Uncle Bert said.

"From where?"

"From here."

"A safe?"

"No. No, not a safe, but a damn stout room, it is."

"Wired?"

"Course it is. Electric eyes and all that. The best. But it didn't bother them none."

"They're pros, they are," Ned Nitry said.

"Is that what the police think?" I said.

"No police, Phil," Eddie Apex said in a flat tone.

"No police," I said, making it a statement rather than a question.

"No," Uncle Norbert said. "No police."

I leaned back in my chair and looked at them. "You said that the man who owns the sword is your client. I may not be going about this in the right way, but I'm going to have to ask you just what the hell kind of business are you in?"

It was Ned Nitry who decided to answer my question, after using an almost imperceptible glance to check it out with his brother. "We specialize in fine works of art," he said. "We sell them on consignment for a modest fee."

"So does Sotheby's," I said, "but they advertise in *The Times*."

"So they do," Uncle Norbert said. "We're more discreet."

"I bet you are," I said. "I bet you're so discreet that the Inland Revenue people don't even know you exist."

Ned Nitry smiled slightly. "I think you're getting the picture, Mr. St. Ives. I think you are indeed. It's a terrible tax burden that the average man must bear up under these days, especially here in England."

"Suppose I had a Thomas Eakins painting," I said.

"You'd be a fortunate man," Ned Nitry said. "Most fortunate."

"Uh-huh. But suppose I was a little short of cash and I wanted to sell it. Of course, I'd have it insured since it was an Eakins."

"I'd hope so, lad, I'd certainly hope so," Ned Nitry said.

"And suppose I wanted to evade paying taxes on the proceeds of the sale. In the states there's a fine line between tax avoidance and tax evasion."

"Is there now?" Uncle Norbert said.

"Tax avoidance is legal; tax evasion isn't."

"Well, I'd say that's wise, wouldn't you, Ned?"

"Absolutely."

"And suppose I came to you with this problem of mine?"

"Well, sir, I think we could be of some assistance," Ned Nitry said. "I do indeed think we could."

"You want to tell me how?"

"Well, I don't think we need go into the details," he said.

"If you don't go into the details, I catch the plane back tonight."

"It's like that, is it?"

"It's like that."

"Tell him, for God's sake, Ned," Eddie Apex said. "He's not stupid."

Ned Nitry nodded a couple of times. "Well, lad, if you

had an Eakins like you say, and you were hard pressed for a bit of cash, and you wanted to sell it discreet like, well, here's what we could do for you. First of all, there's the insurance company to bother about. You've got to keep them happy. They're a gossipy lot and if you just canceled your policy, well, they'd want to know why. And if you kept on paying the premiums on a painting that you'd sold on the sly, so to speak, well, they have those investigators of theirs, you know. But suppose you had a fair likeness of the painting that you wanted to sell?"

"Like the one that's hanging above the mantel in the red room?"

"Like that exactly, sir."

"That's better than a fair likeness," I said. "That's perfect."

Ned Nitry nodded judiciously this time. "It's good enough to satisfy any insurance company I know of."

"And most museums," Eddie Apex said.

"I think you're getting the idea now, aren't you, Mr. St. Ives?" Ceil Apex said.

"I think so," I said.

"Don't you think Dad and Uncle Norbert are terribly wicked?"

"Uh-huh," I said. "Terribly." I looked at Uncle Norbert. "Okay. We've got a phony painting in place to satisfy the insurance company. What next?"

"Well, next is finding you a discreet buyer who'll pay a fair price. That's next."

"And you can do this?"

"We can."

"A cash deal?"

"Of course. And in a Swiss bank, too, if you'd like—or Panama or Beirut, whatever's your pleasure."

"And you charge a commission?"

"A fair commission."

"How much?"

"Thirty percent."

"That's a little more than fair, isn't it?"

58

"We have terrible expenses, lad," Uncle Norbert said. "We have to spirit the painting out of the country usually and get it into another one. We have to commission the fair likeness and, well, you know what dealing with artists is like. They're a bad lot mostly. Drink too much. Get temperamental."

"But they don't talk?"

"We get them in a little too deep to talk. We get them in a little too deep and make them a little too fat. They don't talk."

"Whoever did that Eakins in there is a genius," I said.

"At copying, he is. He's that. But he can't paint an apple on his own without making it look like an orange."

"Let's get back to the sword. You're not going to duplicate that, are you?"

Ned Nitry shook his head. "No need. And nobody even knows it exists except us and our client."

"And the thieves."

"Them, too."

"How'd they find out about it?"

"That's something we'd like to know," Ned Nitry said.

"Any ideas?"

"None."

"Had you already started negotiations for its sale?"

"Only the most delicate kind. A hint or two dropped in the right ear, you might say."

"Whose ear?"

"A representative of the French government."

"You're going to sell it in France?"

"It's a national treasure, lad. It's the Sword of St. Louis and no mistake. Suppose your original Declaration of Independence had been lost for a couple of hundred years and suddenly turned up—in 1976, say—d'you think your government wouldn't spend a few dollars, no questions asked, to get it back?"

"My government?"

"Yes."

"Maybe," I said. "But I'm not too sure. If it were the

original Bill of Rights, you might not get a dime."

"Well, the French are a bit more practical."

"So I've heard." I looked at my watch. "How much are you asking for it?"

"Three million pounds," Uncle Norbert said.

"Jesus."

"They didn't blink an eye."

"But they will," Ned Nitry said. "Those Frenchies like to haggle."

"How much will you come down?" I said.

"Not more'n fifty thousand quid. We might've come down a bit more but this hundred thousand ransom's going to eat into everybody's pocket."

"Are you paying it—or is your client?"

"It was in our possession so we are," Uncle Norbert said. "And it cuts our profit by a tenth, let me tell you."

"Has your client got a name?" I said.

"He does," Ned Nitry said. "Why?"

"Because I'm going to have to talk to him."

"That isn't really necessary, Phil," Eddie Apex said.

"It isn't?"

"No."

I sighed. "Eddie, I'm thinking of going in on a deal that you're in on. And although I think you're a real nice guy and are probably sweet to your lovely wife, I'm not going into any deal that you're in on until I check it out. Do you really blame me?"

Eddie Apex gave me his best grin, the one that was so charmingly honest that it made you want to do something nice for him, such as buying his entire stock of gold bricks. "No," he said. "I don't blame you. If I were dealing with me, I'd do the same thing. His name's Robin Styles. Styles with a y."

"Where can I find him?"

"During the day he moves around a lot. After ten or eleven at night you can always find him at Shields."

"What's Shields?"

"One of our newer gambling hells. It's on Curzon. All the cabbies know it."

"Can I get in?"

Apex nodded. "I'll fix it."

"If you're satisfied after talking to our client, Mr. Styles, does that mean you're in?" Uncle Norbert asked.

"I'm in," I said.

"Not too rich for you, eh?"

"As far as I'm concerned, I'll be helping to restore a national treasure to France. What you do with your money is your concern. I'll pay taxes on mine."

"Well, that's wonderful. Isn't that wonderful, Ned?"

"Wonderful," Ned Nitry said.

"I might need that hundred thousand ransom in a hurry," I said.

"We've got it," Uncle Norbert said.

"Have you got any pictures of the sword?"

Ned Nitry reached into a jacket pocket and handed me an envelope. I took out several color prints that had been taken with a Polaroid. One of them showed Eddie Apex holding the sword out as if he were about to lead the next charge on the Saracens. The others were close-ups of the sword, or at least as close up as the Polaroid could get and still focus. I could see the big diamond in the pommel and the Nitry brothers were right. It was as big as an egg laid by a healthy hen. It didn't look like a diamond to me, but then I'm not too familiar with what rough diamonds look like.

"How do I identify the thing?" I said.

"Identify it?" Uncle Norbert said. He looked puzzled.

"That's right. These pictures are okay, but suppose the thieves found themselves an old swordsmith around who could run them up a fake."

"Not likely," Ned Nitry said.

"I like to be sure."

The Nitry brothers looked at each other. Then Uncle Norbert got up and came around the table to where I sat.

He pointed to the photo that was the best one of the hilt and pommel. "You see right here?" he said, pointing to the hilt just below the pommel.

"Yes."

"Well, get yourself a little magnifying glass. And use it to look right there. You'll see a tiny NN scratched into the gold. But get the glass because you can't see it with the naked eye."

"That sounds as if you'd been expecting something."

Norbert shook his head. "No, lad. It's just habit. We always put our initials on the paintings that we substitute for the real ones so we won't have a mix-up. They just look like scratches on the frames."

I looked at my watch again. It was nearly two-thirty. "Well, I suppose I'd better go back and get to work."

"Doing what?" Uncle Norbert asked.

"Waiting for the phone to ring."

"What if the thieves call before you've seen Styles?"

"I'll stall them until after I talk to him."

"We don't want any slips," Ned Nitry said.

"There won't be any."

"I'll have Tom run you back," Apex said.

I shook my head. "I'd rather walk." I rose. "By the way, Eddie. Where do you fit into the family business?"

He smiled. "I'm the customers man. We go after much of our business, you know. My job is to make ever so discreet calls on the stately homes of England. You'd be surprised at how many fake old masters are hanging on those stately walls. Shocking, really."

"Eddie's a wonderful salesman," his wife said.

"That's because he probably believes in what he's dealing in," I said.

"I deal in what I've always dealt in."

"Greed?" I said.

"That's right," he said. "Greed."

62

Chapter
Nine

*B*ack at the Hilton I made three phone calls, set up two appointments for later that afternoon, and then called down and asked room service to send up some hot chocolate.

While I waited I went over to the window and gazed out at Hyde Park. It looked green and inviting in the May sunshine as did the rest of what I could see of the city from my tenth-story room and I wondered why I had never grown fond of London. I decided that it may have been the language. If they had spoken something incomprehensible such as Bulgarian, I probably would have found it to be all very quaint and charming. But because they spoke English, they should know better, and what would have been quaint in Sofia was only inconvenient in London.

There was a knock at the door and when I opened it, it wasn't the waiter with the chocolate, it was a man of about thirty-five dressed in a dark brown suit with blue shirt, striped tie, brown shoes, and cop written right across his thin, still face.

"Mr. St. Ives?" he said.

"That's right."

"My name's Deskins."

He was about to say something else, but I said, "Not Deskins of Scotland Yard?"

Something started across his face, surprise perhaps, but he caught it and brought it back before it got too far. "It shows, does it?"

"A little. Come in."

He came in and looked around the way that all cops look around in hotel rooms, as if they knew that they could get the goods on you if they could just take a peek under the bed. After that he seemed to make a mental estimate of how much the room cost and then glanced at me as if trying to decide whether I could afford it.

"Would you like to see some identification?" he said.

"No."

"I watch some of the Yank programs on the telly. 'The FBI.' I watch that sometimes. They're always whipping out their identification."

"It's a rule they have," I said.

There was another knock on the door. Deskins almost looked pleased. "Expecting someone?"

"That's right." I opened the door and the waiter wheeled in the hot chocolate in a silver pot that looked as though it held enough for four. Next to it was a plate of those cute little sandwiches with all of the crust sliced off.

"I didn't order the sandwiches," I said.

"No charge, sir. Compliments of the house."

"Thank the house for me," I said and signed the bill, adding enough tip to produce what sounded like a sincere thank you very much, sir, from the waiter.

"Like a cup?" I said to Deskins.

"Tea?"

"Hot chocolate."

"Is it now? I haven't had a cup of chocolate in years."

"Neither have I."

I poured two cups and handed him one. "Have a sandwich," I said, prying up the bread on one to make sure it wasn't tomato. It was ham. Deskins shrugged, picked up one, and took a bite of it. I hoped he had got the tomato. "Missed my lunch," he said.

I took another sandwich, sat down in a chair, and waited. Deskins also took another one and sat down on the bed.

"Well, I'm glad to see you're off the booze, Mr. St. Ives."

"Uh-huh."

"Strange thing, coincidence, isn't it?"

"Uh-huh."

"I was just pulling up to the Magistrates' Court this morning on Marylebone when you came out and hopped into that gray Rolls."

"That's pretty strange, all right."

"So I said to myself, what would an American gentleman be doing coming out of Magistrates' Court at ten in the morning and hopping into Eddie Apex's Rolls?"

"How'd you know I was an American gentleman?"

"It shows."

"I suppose it does."

"So I went in and found out who you were and where you were staying and why you'd been in court. Drunk, you were, they said."

"That's what they said."

"You don't look like a boozer."

"We come in all shapes."

"Well, I'm a bit interested in Eddie Apex and his friends. Have been for years. So I called a colleague of mine in New York."

"You must have a loose budget."

"Not really. He and I've worked together before. I had another matter to talk with him about anyway."

"What's his name?"

"Lieutenant Dontano."

"Fraud squad."

65

"That's right. You know him, don't you?"

"We've met."

"Lieutenant Dontano told me what line of work you're in. I don't think I've ever come across a go-between before —not a professional type who makes a living at it."

"There're a few of us around. Not many, but a few. There's been some talking of forming a union, but so far it's only talk."

He looked at me narrowly with those cop blue eyes of his. "That must be a joke."

"A small one."

He sighed. "I like a good giggle as well as the next, but I'm not much on American humor. I watched that program of yours a time or two on the telly—'Laugh-In,' I think it's called. I had to ask the wife why the people were laughing. She tried to explain it to me, but I still didn't see anything to laugh at."

"I think it's gone off the air."

"No great loss, I'd say."

"Not much."

"Well, Mr. St. Ives, I was wondering if you might tell me what brings you to London and into the company of Eddie Apex?"

"Why don't you ask Eddie?"

"Eddie doesn't talk much, especially to me."

"I'm sorry, but I don't think I can be too cooperative either."

"May I assume that you're working?"

"You can assume anything you want."

"You know Eddie rather well, don't you?"

"I once interviewed him for a paper that I worked for."

"Then you know what he is."

"I know what he was. He was a confidence man."

"Was?"

"He retired."

"Did he now?"

"That's what he told me."

Deskins finished his hot chocolate. "Well, I suppose you met the missus?"

"Whose?"

"Eddie's."

"I met her."

"I see old Tom's still driving for Eddie. Did you meet Jack?"

"The butler?"

"Yes."

"I saw him."

"Still getting about, is he?"

"Seems to be."

"I suppose old Jack would be long before your time, unless you made a study of such things."

"What things?"

"Famous thieves, for example. Know much about them?"

"A little."

"Ever hear of a Gentleman Jack Brooks?"

"You're kidding. That old man?"

Deskins nodded. "That's him. Worked the Riviera before the first war. New York in the twenties. Mayfair any time. Probably the best jewel thief who ever lived. Slowed down when he got to be fifty. They caught him coming out of Brown's in the summer of forty-three dressed up in a general's uniform and his pockets stuffed with some Indian nabob's jewel case. A fortune in diamonds, I'm told. They also tell me that old Jack certainly looked the part. Of a general, I mean."

"What happened?"

"To Jack? He did ten straight without remission at Wormwood Scrubs. When he got out he went to work as a butler for the Nitry brothers. Have you met Eddie's father-in-law, Ned Nitry?"

"We met."

"And Uncle Bert?"

I nodded.

"They're a pair," he said. "Bent out of shape if ever I saw. Know how they got started?"

"No."

"They damn near ran the black market in the East End during the war. Those two and a couple of American captains who supplied them. Sugar, tea, coffee, beef, stockings, chocolate—they had the lot. Sold it by the ton, I'm told, and made a fortune."

"They ever get caught?"

"Never. They spread it around too thick to get caught, if you know what I mean."

"I think so," I said. "What happened after the war?"

"To the Nitrys? It went a treat after the war. For them, at least. They invested everything in West End property, moved to Knightsbridge, and even hired old Tom when he got out of the nick."

"Tom," I said. "You mean Eddie's chauffeur."

"Back in the late twenties and early thirties he was a race driver. Raced anything—bikes, cars, what have you. He raced in Europe mostly. Then in the late thirties, I'd have to say that old Tom fell among evil companions. A smash-and-grab gang working out of Soho. He was their driver, their wheelman, I think you'd call him, and probably the best ever."

"What happened to him?"

"He got caught one night when a tire went. He spent the war and then some in the Scrubs, too. When he got out, who should hire old Tom Bates but Ned and Norbert Nitry."

"They sound like real humanitarians."

"Mmm," Deskins said and rose from the bed. He looked at me with his frosty blue eyes that somehow went with that still, thin face and its tight mouth, worried frown, fox nose, and a chin that I could hang my hat on. "I'm not here to tell you who you should be keeping company with, Mr. St. Ives. But I don't mind telling you that the Nitry brothers are a nasty lot."

"I'll keep that in mind," I said.

He reached into a pocket and handed me a card. "If you think of something interesting that you'd like to tell me, ring this number." I looked at the card. There was nothing on it but his name, William Deskins, and a telephone number.

"All right," I said. "If I think of something interesting."

He moved to the door and opened it. "Good-bye, Mr. St. Ives. And thank you very much for the chocolate."

"Not at all," I said.

When he was gone I went over to the phone and called the number that was on the card. There were two double rings and when a voice answered, a man's voice, with a snappy, "Fifth Division, Constable Akers," I hung up.

Chapter
Ten

*W*hen my former wife and I had lived in London that year at the very beginning of the 1960s, when all fine things had seemed possible, even my becoming sort of a wisecracking Walter Lippmann, I had grown knowledgeable and even authoritative on a number of things English such as clotted cream, Parliament, the Royal Family, Lyons Corner Houses, and the London Underground. Having got the underground down cold, I had set out to master the city's bus system only to fall back in utter confusion after a couple of weeks.

But the underground had remained my specialty and I had delighted in giving detailed, even painstaking instructions to visiting Americans on how they could best go down to Kew in lilac time, or east to Upminster on the District Line, or west to Uxbridge on the Piccadilly, or even the Metropolitan.

The first appointment that I had made for that afternoon was at an address that I vaguely recalled as being on the dingier outskirts of Maida Vale. So just to kill time and determine whether I still retained my London tube lore I strolled through Mayfair to Oxford Circus and caught the Bakerloo Line to the Maida Vale station where a news vendor told me that 99 Ashworth Road wasn't far at all, just a couple of streets down Elgin Avenue and to my right.

As a neighborhood, Elgin Avenue was on the skids. There was a two-block stretch of funky-looking shops and then, to the west, row after row of red brick flats that seemed bent on nudging each other toward slum status although it might be another ten years before they all got there.

Ashworth Road was a little better. It was a short street lined with trees and well-tended gardens and prim-looking semidetached houses that probably were built just before the first world war. It was a quiet neighborhood, for some reason too quiet, until I realized that there was none of the stuff that normally serves to gauge a residential neighborhood's vitality. There were no abandoned tricycles on the walk, or forgotten teddy bears, or waiting prams. It was a street without children, a street of drawn curtains, bolted doors, and aging but well-dusted cars, including a small Bentley that I guessed to be at least forty years old.

I decided that it was a street from which the young had fled while the old stayed on. I was its lone pedestrian that afternoon as I walked down the cracked sidewalk, the leather heels of my black loafers banging out into that quiet that belonged in a small town, not a big city. As I walked I thought I could detect the rustle of a drawn curtain here and there and I assumed that suspicious old eyes were watching to see what house I stopped at. I may have been that month's excitement on Ashworth Road.

Roses were the flowers there. Dark red roses that nodded in the warm May afternoon from behind chest-high brick walls and iron fences. They were the only friendly thing in sight and the front yard of the house at 99 Ashworth Road had its full share of them.

It was hard to tell how old he was, the man who answered my knock. He could have been a desiccated fifty or a not bad seventy. His was a dried, pinched face, tight and somehow unforgiving, and so deeply wrinkled that I wondered how he shaved.

"St. Ives," he said, as if calling some long forgotten roll. And then after a pause, "Philip."

"That's right," I said instead of present. "Doctor Christenberry?"

He nodded and started to open the door wider, but thought better of it. "You understand about the consultation fee?"

"Ten guineas."

"Yes. That's correct. Ten guineas." He opened the door just wide enough for me to slip past him. He wore old, stained gray flannel trousers, carpet slippers, a gray coat sweater that was buttoned up wrong, and a tieless shirt that may have been white at one time, but which was now a sort of grayish yellow. He said, "How do you do?" as I came in and I noticed that he smelled.

The man whom the smell belonged to was Julian Christenberry and he had his doctorate from Heidelberg plus an M.A. and a F.S.A. from somewhere else, and according to the Assistant to the Master of the Armouries at the Tower of London, Doctor Julian Christenberry knew more than anyone else in the world about medieval armor and weaponry, unless I went to Oakeshott, who unfortunately was no longer available.

The small foyer that I found myself in was furnished with two stiff chairs, three awful paintings, and four suits of plate armor that stood stiffly about not doing much of anything other than collecting dust, except for the one whose right mailed fist held an old black hat, a gray scarf, and an umbrella.

"I think we'll be more comfortable in here," Christenberry said and pushed through a door that led to a sitting room that turned out to be a dim place with drawn curtains, one lighted floor lamp, and the kind of furniture that you would expect to find on Ashworth Road. Two lumpy-looking, overstuffed chairs hunched toward a fireplace that contained an electric heater. There was a couch slipcovered in a faded, flowery print. A dull brown rug covered most of the floor. A massive desk faced the curtained windows and was littered with pieces of paper that looked like bills. Here and there, rickety tables held big vases choked with roses.

Except for the walls, the room and its furniture seemed to be much like the man who lived there, worn and used up, not quite good enough to sell but not bad enough to throw out. The walls, however, were covered with items designed to bash heads, break bones, sever limbs, and knock out teeth. There were swords of all kinds, long ones and short ones, wide and thin, curved, straight, and wiggly. There were wicked daggers and stout war axes. There were harpins and catchpoles and partizans and halberds and poleaxes. There were maces and spiked flails and cudgels and even a caltrop or two.

It was quite a collection and I told Christenberry so. He nodded and smiled with yellow teeth. "And all designed with a single purpose," he said. "To hurt. To maim. To kill." The idea seemed to please him momentarily—until he thought of something less cheerful. "Unfortunately," he said, "I've had to sell off the really good pieces. One by one I've sold them off to provide a bit of bread and meat for my table."

I felt that I could take a hint as well as anyone so I brought out my wallet and handed him two five-pound notes along with a fifty-pence piece. "Ten guineas," I said.

He pocketed the money hurriedly, apparently afraid that I might change my mind. "I suppose you'll take tea?" he said, as if trying to be gracious, but knowing that he wasn't very good at it.

74

"If it's no bother."

There were some tea things and an electric kettle on a table next to one of the lumpy armchairs and he started fooling around with them. On a plate by the kettle were four vanilla cookies, one of which had pink icing. The kettle was already starting to whistle and he gestured me to the chair opposite him. He took a single tea bag, dropped it into the pot, and then poured in what seemed to be about four cups of water. We sat there and waited for it to steep. He had his eyes half closed and his mouth half open and I wasn't sure whether he was about to say something or doze off.

"You're a journalist, are you?" he said after a while.

"A reporter."

"What paper did you say you worked for?"

"I didn't say, but it's *The New York Times*." I crossed my legs elegantly, the way that I thought a *Times* man might.

"Hmm," he said. "They should be able to afford ten guineas. No need to feel sorry for them."

"No need," I said.

He twisted to his left and poured the tea. "What do you take?" he said.

"Sugar. One lump."

He passed me my cup. Then he offered the plate of four cookies. "Biscuit?"

"No, thank you."

He seemed relieved. He snatched up the one with the pink icing and crammed it into his mouth, chewing noisily.

I sipped my tea. It was weak. "Very good," I said.

"You mentioned over the telephone that you were interested in medieval weaponry," he said. "Don't know why you should be. No one else is today."

"I'm putting together an article on some of the lost and missing treasures of the world which lately seem to be popping up. For instance, about three years ago the Boston Museum of Fine Arts suddenly acquired a gaggle

75

of gold treasures from the Bronze Age, from Turkey probably. Then there was that Raphael portrait of the Duchess of Urbino that the same museum got and had to give back to Italy. More recently has been the uproar concerning what they're calling the Great Calyx Krater mystery. That was the Greek vase done by the Athenian artist Euphronius. It went for a million dollars and turned up in the Metropolitan Museum of Art in New York."

"Can't see how any of this has to do with armor," Christenberry said.

"I'm coming to that, if you'll bear with me. What we'd like to do is to anticipate some of the treasures that might pop up. The Peking Man, for example. That disappeared in China just after Pearl Harbor. Now there's talk that it might turn up any day."

"Not much interested in paintings," Christenberry said. "Ignorant about them really. Greek pots, too. I seem to recall that the Peking Man's nothing but old bones."

"But priceless," I said.

"Can't see why. The world's nothing but a graveyard filled with old bones."

"That's just one example," I said. "We've also heard rumors that several other lost or missing items are about to surface. They're just rumors though and I'm trying to check them out. For instance, I've got a line on somebody who claims to know the whereabouts of the crown of the Infante Fernando. Another lead I have to follow up on is that somebody's holding the gold and silver shield of Ruy Diaz de Bivar. You know, El Cid."

"I know," Christenberry said drily.

"I thought you might," I said. "And then there's another persistent rumor that keeps cropping up about something called the Sword of St. Louis."

I watched him as I spun my tale. His lips had twisted themselves into what I took to be a sneer until I got to the Sword of St. Louis. Then they clamped themselves

76

down into a line so tightly closed that I thought I might have to pry it open.

But after a moment he sipped his tea and popped another cookie into his mouth. "You are off on the wrong track, young man. Indeed you are."

"How?"

"The Infante Fernando had no crown. I'll spare you the details, but if you'd done any research at all, you'd know that. There was no crown."

"All right," I said.

"As for the Cid having a shield of silver and gold, that's utter rot. He was a fighting man and an excellent one. He certainly wouldn't have burdened himself with an overly elaborate shield. Where could you have heard such rubbish?"

"Around," I said. "What about the Sword of St. Louis? Is that rubbish, too?"

Those thin lips clamped themselves together again. He had wet gray eyes, as nervous as quicksilver, and they darted around the room as though looking for the escape hatch until they finally lit on something—something reassuring, I thought, a Basilard dagger perhaps.

"It was a bastard sword," he said in a low voice.

"A what?"

"A bastard sword. That meant that it had a hand-and-a-half hilt. One could wield it with one hand or both, if the action called for it. Fine steel, too, it was. Not razor sharp, of course; none of them was, but it took an edge that can't be matched on any of today's knives."

"So it existed," I said.

"Oh, yes. Yes, indeed. There's no doubt of that. It's far too well authenticated."

"Including the diamond as big as an egg in the pommel?"

His eyes started skittering around the room again. "So you've heard that, have you?" he said, not looking at me.

"I've heard."

"Rock crystal most likely, if that. Swords were damned democratic things in medieval times. There was a brotherhood then among knights which made the simplest of them the equal of kings. A knight was as good as his sword and not many indulged themselves in fancy trimmings."

"So you don't believe there was a diamond?"

"If Louis had had a diamond as large as you claim, he probably would have used it to help finance his Crusades."

"Maybe it was his mad money," I said.

"I beg your pardon?"

"His emergency fund. Maybe he kept it tucked away in the hilt of his sword."

Christenberry tried on his yellow smile again. He didn't wear it well. "I suppose we'll never find out though, will we?"

"I don't know," I said. "I hear that the thing's turned up here in London."

"Impossible," he said. "I would have heard."

"That's what I thought. I heard that it went for twelve-and-six in a shop on Shaftesbury Avenue back in thirty-nine and that the present owner just recently found out what he had."

"Twelve-and-six," the old man whispered. "My God, twelve-and-six."

"How much do you think it would be worth now?" I said. "With the diamond."

He shook his head. "Priceless," he said.

"Nothing's priceless, Doctor Christenberry. The Rosetta Stone's only insured for a million pounds."

He shrugged. He wasn't really listening to me. He was thinking of the bargain that had gone for twelve-and-six on Shaftesbury Avenue in 1939. "Two million pounds," he said. "Three million perhaps. The French would pay three million. *Twelve-and-six!* Oh, dear God, think of it. Twelve-and-six. They didn't tell me that." He looked up sharply to see if I had heard.

78

"How much did they pay you?" I said.

"Who?"

"I don't know who. But how much did they pay you to authenticate it?"

His wet eyes went roaming again. "I'm a poor man. The world pays you nothing while you work and then it pensions you off with a pittance and oh, God, I get so hungry sometimes why can't I just die." He was starting to snuffle. He pulled at his nose a couple of times. It was the only unwrinkled spot on his face except his eyes, and if they had seemed wet before, they were flooded now.

"They wanted you to authenticate the sword, didn't they?" I said.

"Yes," he said between snuffles.

"Did you?"

He waved an angry arm. "I don't have the proper equipment anymore. I sold it. I told them that. They said they'd be satisfied with just my opinion. They said I knew more about the sword than anybody else and God knows they were right. I spent years and years and a tidy sum ferreting out every scrap of information there was about the wretched thing. Years I spent and now you tell me that it went for twelve-and-six." His voice rose. "I could have been there! I could have been there in Shaftesbury Avenue that very day. Oh, God, why wasn't it me?"

"And was it what they thought it was?" I said.

Some hiccups interrupted his snuffles. But he nodded anyway. Then he stretched out his hands. "I held it right here—right in these very hands."

"How much did they pay you?"

The hiccups and snuffles died away. "My pension. They paid me a sum equal to my pension for a year. Five hundred pounds. That's what I have to starve on. Isn't that a princely sum?"

I took out my wallet again. He watched me. I counted out five ten-pound notes onto the arm of my lumpy chair. He watched that, too.

"Who were they?" I said.

He licked his lips as though he could taste the ten-pound notes. "You're going to give me that money, if I tell you?"

"That's right."

"They swore me to secrecy."

I sighed, took the wallet out again, and added another ten-pound note to the pile.

"Was the diamond in the pommel?" I said.

He nodded.

"Who were they?"

He shook his head. "I don't know. They were two men. They wouldn't tell me their names."

"Young or old?"

"Younger than I—but getting on. In their sixties, I'd say."

"Did they look alike?"

He nodded. "They could have been brothers. One was harder looking than the other."

"And you got a good look at the sword?"

"I spent two hours on it. Two lovely hours. It was in surprisingly good condition. Much better than I'd have expected."

"Anything else about it? Anything unusual?"

He shook his head. "No, not really. Except on the hilt just below the pommel. I didn't see it until I used the glass. It looked as if somebody had scratched his initials into it—into the gold."

"Were the initials NN?"

He looked surprised. "Yes, they were. Now may I have my money?"

I rose and handed it to him. "Thank you, Doctor Christenberry. You've been a lot of help. I'll find my way out."

I don't think he really heard me. He was already counting the money. I went through the door into the foyer and closed it. Then I opened and closed the door that led to the street, but I went back and pressed my ear against the thin panel of the foyer door. I didn't have to wait. He was already dialing the phone.

"This is Christenberry," he said. "He only just left. I told him what you told me to tell him. Now may I have my money?"

I slipped out the front door and walked up to Elgin Avenue, caught a taxi, gave the driver an address on Harley Street, and thought about what I had heard and overheard in the house at 99 Ashworth Road. As I thought about it, I decided that it may have been what I was supposed to have overheard.

Chapter
Eleven

*I*f you are good enough and, for all I know, smooth enough, you can join the Royal College of Surgeons, hang out your shingle on Harley Street, and call yourself Mister instead of Doctor, which is the same logic that the British fell back on when they started calling their private schools public.

I had met Daniel Defoe about a dozen years before, just after he had opened his office on Harley Street and started calling himself Mr and sending out his bills in nice round guinea figures. I had met him at an all-night poker game where he had informed me that yes, he was descended from the writer; that he was Defoe's great-great-great nephew or something, and that no, he didn't believe that I had filled my flush. He had been right and he had won nearly enough in that particular pot to furnish his reception room. He also had become our family doctor, if Harley Streeters can be considered such, and my former wife had gone to him several times for various mild complaints while I had gone to him once with an ingrown toenail, just to make sure that he didn't lose the common touch.

We hadn't seen each other for three or four years, not since the last time he had been in New York, and so we spent fifteen minutes catching up on whatever gossip we still had in common and in my admiring his newly decorated consultation room.

"I can see that a lot of thought as well as a few buckets of tonsils went into all this," I said. "You driving a Rolls yet?"

He smiled. He could charge an extra five guineas for that smile alone. "Since last year, I call it my Vasectomy V-8."

"You do a lot of those?"

"I've suddenly become the bloody authority. It's a two- or three-quid operation, you know. But nobody wants that. There's something about the family jewels that demands the expert's touch. So I pop them into hospital overnight, in a private room, of course, snip away for five minutes, send them a bill for a hundred guineas, and they're delighted. I did more than two hundred of the things last year. Quite a few chaps from Scotland Yard for some reason."

"Cops get a lot of free ass," I said.

"Do they really?"

"They say they do anyway."

Mr Defoe looked at me. It was his diagnostic look, I thought. He had a handsome, strongboned face, the kind that women adore and men don't mind. His eyes were a large dark brown with a hint of pain in their depths, which all fine doctors have, and even some bad ones. His hair was carefully tousled and getting just a little gray and I found myself wishing that I had something wrong with me that he could take a look at. A bad hangnail would do.

"Are you over here on holiday or are you on one of those odd jobs that you do now and again?" he said.

"I'm working."

He smiled once more. "Does it hurt?"

"Only in the mornings when I have to get up."

"I suppose I should envy you, Philip, but I still like what I'm doing so marvelously well that I don't have time."

"I don't want to take up any more of it," I said. "Although I thought we might have dinner before I go back."

"Or a game," he said.

"If you can round up some fish."

"No trouble. What else is on your mind?"

"Somebody slipped something into my drink the other day."

"What happened?"

"Cramps. Then nausea followed by a terrific high. Euphoria, really. Then I blacked out."

"You weren't drinking a great deal, were you?"

"It was my only drink all day."

"What was it, Scotch?"

"Yes."

"Did you notice any taste?"

I thought back. "It might have tasted a little bitter, but I'm not sure."

"How much do you smoke now?"

I shrugged. "Three packs a day."

"Dear God! What *can* you taste?"

"Salt. I can taste salt."

"Well, I can tell you what it could have been, although I can't be certain."

"Of course."

"Morphine."

"Would that do it?"

He nodded. "I think thirty milligrams—a half-grain—might do it and you might not notice it if the Scotch were bad and the taste buds ruined, as yours seem to be. You wouldn't have built up any tolerance for it either and that could have produced the symptoms you described."

"I was just curious."

"Did you like it?"

"What?"

"The euphoria."

"Sure," I said. "I was crazy about it."

Mr Daniel Defoe nodded gloomily. "I was afraid you might be," he said.

At eleven o'clock that night the deep voice behind me said, "Well, well, well, well, well, *well*. If it isn't Philip St. Ives, the honest messenger boy." He made me sound like an Horatio Alger novel. The worst one.

I turned. He was still as tall as he had always been, around six-foot-seven, but a lot heavier, at least 250 or 275 pounds. It's hard to guess accurately when it gets up that high.

His name was Wesley Cagle and his chief claim to fame was that he had once played football for Princeton and later the St. Louis Cardinals. Tight end, I think, but he hadn't been much good as a pro and had lasted only two seasons. Years back, I had done a column on him when he had gone to work for Meyer Lansky as a "public relations consultant." He hadn't liked the column much, which was probably because I hadn't liked him much, and it had showed.

"You're fat, Wes," I said because it was the first nasty thing that came to mind.

He slapped his gut which bulged against the studs of his dress shirt. He wore his dinner jacket well, which is something that few really big men can do without looking like an extra waiter. "Only a few pounds," he said. "They give me a touch of dignity, which is something this joint can use."

I looked around. Shields Gambling Emporium was a gaudy, glittering place with rows of heavy chandeliers, lots of red plush, dark mahogany, brass spittoons, and anything else that would make it look as though it had begun operation in 1894. In the background I could hear the gambling sounds: the slap of cards, the croupiers' drone, the spinning balls, and the clicking chips.

"What do you do here, Wes, shave the dice?"

"I'm what is known as the deputy managing director." He made a small bow. "Welcome to Shields, Mr. St. Ives, and I hope you lose your teeth. Drink?"

"Why not?"

We went over to a bar where a well-dressed gray-haired man stood, a drink in his hand, and tears streaming down his cheeks. I moved farther on down the bar and Cagle followed.

We ordered drinks and Cagle nodded toward the gray-haired man at the bar. "He dropped a thousand that he doesn't have or can't afford so I bought him a drink."

"Well, that's what you get for going to Princeton. Decent instincts."

The fat hadn't yet reached Cagle's face. It was still mostly planes and angles and handsome enough if you don't mind a thrice-broken nose. When he smiled, I saw that he had either had his teeth capped or had got some brand new ones.

"I got a call about you today," he said. "From an old friend."

"It must have been one of mine then. You don't have any friends. Not old ones anyhow." I don't know why I needled him. He seemed to be trying to be nice and if he got tired of that, he could always hammer me into the rug with one hand.

"English Eddie Apex," Cagle said.

"Good old Eddie."

"Eddie said to give you the run of the place."

"Did he say anything about credit?"

"He said you could use your own money. He also said that there's somebody here that you might want to meet. Robin Styles."

I nodded. "Is he here?"

"He's always here," Cagle said.

"Does he win or lose?"

Cagle made his big hand go palm up then palm down a few times, indicating that Robin Styles, the man who owned what might turn out to be a three-million-pound sword, did a little of both. But mostly lost.

"How much is he into you?" I said.

"We don't give credit."

I sighed. "Why do you still try to lie to me, Wes, when you know that I know better?"

"It's privileged information."

"Funny, but I just happened to remember something," I said. "I remember a story about what happened between you and Meyer in the Bahamas. It's a hell of a funny story. I don't think too many people know it. I wonder if the guys who own this place have heard it?"

Wes Cagle looked around the bar. "They don't know about the Bahamas. All they know about is Vegas. I was strictly kosher in Vegas."

"They don't have to know about the Bahamas then, do they?"

Cagle let me look at his new teeth again, but he wasn't feeling smilish. "Styles's into us for forty-three thousand pounds. His cutoff is fifty and from the way he's going he might get there tonight."

"What's his game?"

"Seven-card. Nothing else."

"Why're you so lavish with the credit?"

"We're betting on the come," Cagle said, staring at me. "That's what you're betting on, isn't it?"

"Sure," I said. "We go-betweens are just like gambling hells. All heart. You've got a guarantor, Wes, or you wouldn't let Styles bet a dime. Who it is, Eddie Apex?"

"Eddie might have mentioned something about it. That the kid would be okay for up to fifty thou. He also mentioned that you'd want to meet him."

"I'd rather watch him play poker for a while first."

"Uh-huh. Eddie said you'd want to do that, too."

"What kind of game is it?"

"Table stakes."

"Five hundred get me in?"

"Five hundred what?"

"Dollars."

"No, but you could get in for a thousand bucks maybe, if you still play that same tight-assed poker of yours."

"You take a check?"

"Sure, Phil," he said, smiling for the first time as though he meant it. "Traveler's checks."

I took out my book of American Express fifties and started signing away. When I had signed enough, I tore them out and handed them to Wes Cagle. "The table will give you your chips," he said. "I'll point Styles out to you."

"Okay."

"One more thing, Phil."

"What?"

He smiled again, another happy one. "I hope you lose every fucking cent."

Chapter Twelve

I had stayed in my room at the Hilton until ten forty-five that night waiting for somebody to call and tell me where I should bring £100,000. When they didn't, I had walked down to Shields on Curzon Street to take a look at Robin Styles, the young man who owned an old sword that might turn out to be worth a few million pounds.

I had been looking at him for almost five hours now across the green baize of the horseshoe-shaped table. I had decided that since he talked like a twit, drank like a twit, and played poker like a twit, he must be a twit. It was an opinion I was not to change until it was almost too late.

We were playing seven-card stud and the house dealt. There were six of us playing: Styles, a German from Düsseldorf, another Englishman, an American from Dallas, me, and a London type whom I took to be a shill because he looked bored out of his mind and at the stakes we were playing for, it's hard to be bored if it's your very own money that's being won and lost.

"Mr. St. Ives," the man from Dallas said. "I do believe you're tryin' to run another shitty on us, if you'll pardon the expression."

"No need to apologize," I said. "Just bet."

I had been running shitties for the past hour, betting extravagantly on nothing and getting caught at it and betting the same on kings full, which is a pretty fair hand even in seven-card stud, and suckering them all in. I was better than even, and now that I had done my advertising, I was ready to play some mean poker, which is the only way to play it, especially seven-card stud, a game that I had always detested.

I had paired fours on the first two down cards, hit another four on the third up card, and caught the final four buried on the last card down. The German I figured for a high straight, Styles for a flush, and the Texan for a full house. The shill had folded as had the other player who, apropos of nothing, had suddenly announced that he was from Manchester. We had all congratulated him.

The Texan bet first because he had the only pair showing, queens. He bet thirty pounds and everybody called, but when it got around to me I raised him a hundred. Although I had absolutely nothing showing, from the look in the eyes of the man from Dallas, I could see that he had felt the sandbag fall. A superb professional gambler would simply have yawned and folded his full house. A gifted amateur probably would have called and let it go at that. A good Saturday night player, riding his luck, would have raised me a hundred pounds and that's what the Dallasonian did. I suppose you call the citizens of Dallas Dallasonians. Or Dallasites. I've never really thought about it.

The German, who had been a cool player up until now, fidgeted in his seat, said shit in French, and folded. Robin Styles, who may have been one of the ten worst poker players I've ever seen, raised the Texan's bet by another hundred pounds. This time I dumped the whole truckload of sand on them. I had a little more than five hundred pounds in chips sitting in front of me so I counted them methodically into the pot.

"I'll see the two hundred raise and raise three hundred," I said.

The Texan stared at me. After a while he said, "If you were from London, Mr. St. Ives, I just might believe you and cut and run. But since you're from New York, and everybody knows that folks from New York'll lie like snakes, well, I'm just obliged to call." He shoved in his chips.

I looked at Robin Styles. "I'm afraid I really don't believe you either, Mr. St. Ives," he said and counted his chips into the pot. It wiped him out, which was what I had been waiting for.

"No raises?" I said.

"No raises," said the man from Dallas.

I flipped over my hole cards. "Four fours."

"Mighty fine hand," the Texan said and tossed his cards to the dealer.

"Jolly good," Styles said. As I've mentioned, he sometimes seemed to talk like a twit.

I estimated that there was close to three thousand pounds in the pot. I shoved it toward the dealer and said, "Have these cashed in for me, will you, please? And take twenty pounds for your trouble."

"Thank you very much," he said.

"I always like to quit a little ahead," I said.

The Texan yawned and stretched, which is what he should have done before, instead of calling me. "It's the best time," he said.

Robin Styles sat frowning at the green baize as if trying to decide whether he should exhaust the rest of his credit that night or wait until the following evening.

"Why don't you join me for some breakfast, Mr. Styles?" I said.

He looked up. "Breakfast?" He said it the way he might have said a strange and difficult foreign word. "Well, yes,

I suppose I really should eat, shouldn't I? I mean the condemned man, the hearty breakfast, and all that."

"I'll treat," I said.

"Oh, thank you very much. I could rather do with a drink though."

"I think that can be arranged."

He brightened. "Really? How nice."

Robin Styles was blond and fair-skinned and tall and thin to the point of either emaciation or elegance. His movements were languid and his speech was drawled to the point of affectation and interspersed with frequent "mmm's" which could be taken, I assumed, to mean anything from "right on" to "how terribly nice." I decided that their use must have saved him much time and thought.

After playing six or seven hours of poker, he rose, gave his dark, striped tie a tug, smiled brilliantly, and managed to look as if he had just finished getting all spruced up for a big night out. I suspected that I must have looked as though I should have been buried a few days.

We moved into the lobby where Wes Cagle was leaning against the bar which had been closed since eleven-thirty in accordance with the strange native customs. I had joined the poker game at ten past eleven and between then and the time that the bar closed, Robin Styles had managed to down four very large whiskies. As I said, he drank the same way that he played poker. Like a twit.

Cagle looked up from a sheet of paper that he was studying. Like Styles, he looked no worse for the wear. Or it may have been that he had put on a fresh shirt. He grinned at us and said, "Well, I see that you two have met."

"Mr. St. Ives is going to give me breakfast. I think breakfast is a perfectly splendid idea, don't you, Wes?"

"You took another bath, I hear," Cagle said.

"Indeed I did."

"And you got lucky," he said to me.

"You call it luck; I call it skill."

"We haven't played poker in a long time, have we, Phil?"

"A long time," I agreed.

"It was up in your place on Thirty-fourth Street in that apartment-hotel where all the fags and the high class whores live. And you."

"The Adelphi," I said.

"Yeah. The Adelphi. It was you, me, an actor, that fat millionaire friend of yours, and a couple of boys from the vice squad. I came out of there with close to two thousand bucks."

"I think it was nearer to fifteen hundred."

"Uh-huh. If you're going to be in town a while, why don't you and I play a little head-to-head? No limit. Personal checks accepted."

"I'll think about it."

"I say, could I play, too?" Styles said.

Cagle looked at him. "You can watch. We might even let you go out for sandwiches. You can watch and you might learn something."

Robin Styles smiled. I thought I could detect a measure of pain in that smile, the kind of pain that comes from self-knowledge that has been purchased at a stiff price. For some reason, he no longer looked nearly so much like a twit. "I suppose I could take a few pointers," he said.

"Yeah," Cagle said. "A few."

"Let's go," I said to Styles.

As we left, Cagle called after me. "Just tell 'em where you won it, Phil." It was the old Las Vegas call and for some reason it didn't seem to go over too well in London.

Styles and I walked up Curzon Street toward Park Lane. "Where do you think we should go for breakfast?" he said. "There's a Golden Egg open on Edgware Road, if you can abide them."

"I think we'd better go to my hotel, if you want that drink," I said.

"I don't wish to disappoint you, but I really should tell you. I'm not queer."

"You're not, huh?"

"No."

"You don't disappoint me."

"That's not to say that I've never tried it, you understand. It's simply that I just didn't care for it. Very much."

"You sure you've got my name right?" I said.

"I'm really dreadful with names. St. Ives, isn't it? Philip St. Ives?"

"Eddie Apex didn't mention me to you?"

"Oh, you're *that* Philip St. Ives. I don't mean that, of course. I mean that you're the American that Eddie told me about. I don't think he ever mentioned your name."

"Yeah. Well, I'm the American he told you about."

"The go-between, so to speak."

"So to speak."

"Well, I say, that is jolly good, isn't it?"

I sighed. "I was kind of hoping you'd find it so."

Of all the myths that continue to flourish in England in the face of modern scientific investigation, no myth remains quite so healthy as the one that envelops the English breakfast. This myth cunningly acknowledges that while lunch in England might be a failure and dinner a disaster, the typical English breakfast is fit for, if not a king, at least a fairly solvent duke.

I have eaten English breakfasts in quaint country inns, in sleek hotels, on once crack trains, and in hearty restaurants from Land's End to John O'Groats. In the interest of science, I have always ordered the same breakfast, a high cholesterol number consisting of two fried eggs, bacon, toast, and coffee.

Although price and ambience might vary, the quality has remained steadfastly the same. Awful. The eggs are all fried in an inch or two of old grease. The bacon is underdone. The toast is stone cold. The coffee is unspeakable. But the myth of the English breakfast endures, indeed flourishes, and I have reluctantly concluded that it will long outlive Arthur and his round table. On second thought, I really shouldn't say anything about the toast.

It's supposed to be cold. The natives like it that way. If it's hot, it might soak up the butter. And the butter isn't bad.

It had taken a healthy bribe to have the Hilton deliver two breakfasts up to my room at five in the morning, but they eventually arrived and I sat there looking at mine and making another mental footnote for the exposé that I would write some day. Robin Styles was happily chewing away on his and washing it down with large swallows of straight Scotch.

"Nothing quite like an English breakfast, is there?" he said.

"Nothing."

"The Hilton does it quite well, for an American hotel, I mean."

"They haven't missed a trick," I said.

He forked the last morsel of a hard-fried egg into his mouth and took another swallow of Scotch. "You're in a rather curious sort of business, aren't you?"

"Sort of," I said and began eating my own breakfast on the theory that it might possibly be good for me.

"You don't limit yourself to purloined swords, I take it?"

"No. I'm available for almost anything that can be ransomed. People, jewels, incriminating documents, rare artifacts, missing evidence, old love letters."

"How fascinating. What's the strangest item that you had to do whatever it is that you do to get back?"

I thought about it. "A ferris wheel, I guess."

"You're joking."

"No. A guy once stole a ferris wheel just outside of Baltimore. He couldn't sell it so he offered to ransom it back for a few thousand. There wasn't much money in it for me, but then it didn't take much time."

"You could play poker for a living."

I shook my head. "Poker's hard work, if you want to make a living at it. I don't much care for hard work."

"I don't play very well, you know."

"I know."

"You think I could learn?"

I studied him for a moment. "If you learned how to play well, you probably wouldn't like it, and you'd quit."

He took another swallow of Scotch. "I've tried to quit."

"Couldn't?"

He shook his head. "Compulsion, I suppose." He shrugged. "Perhaps I should take your advice and learn how to play well so I could quit."

"It's hard work, as I said. You have to learn the odds, learn to memorize what cards have been played, read the other players, and wait. Waiting is what makes it dull."

"You make the cure sound worse than the disease."

"It might be in your case. There aren't any halfway houses for compulsive gamblers. There's no tapering off. You either quit cold or you keep on gambling until it's all gone and you take something that doesn't belong to you so that you can gamble one last game and then they catch you and put you away where it's not so easy to gamble anymore. I've never heard of any compulsive gamblers dying either rich or old."

Robin Styles poured another two ounces of Scotch into his glass. "I saw a doctor about it a few times. A psychiatrist. He was a Jungian, I believe."

"He'd be supportive anyway."

"We didn't get anywhere."

"Well, when they sell that sword of yours you should have enough to keep you in chips for a year or two."

"It's such an awful lot of money, isn't it?"

"What did you do for money before?"

"I was in advertising for a while," he said. "I was really rather good at it. It was an American firm." He mentioned the name of a large New York-based agency.

"That's a Wellington tie you're wearing, isn't it?" I said.

He looked surprised. "However did you know?"

"I once did a couple of columns on old school ties. After Wellington, it was Oxford, wasn't it? Balliol, I'll bet."

"I say, does it show?"

I shook my head. "No, it's just that that agency that you

used to work for liked Balliol men to handle some of their stuffier accounts. The clients found them soothing."

"It was a rather good job."

"Why'd you quit?"

"The usual gambler's reasons. I got lucky and won as much in a week as I made in a year. So I quit."

"How'd you meet Eddie Apex?"

"Through Wes Cagle at Shields. I was stony. My father had left me this sword collection plus just enough to get through school so I thought I might sell the collection. I'd heard somewhere that such things could be sold on the quiet without the tax people looking over your shoulder. So I asked Cagle if he knew anyone who could help. He said he would see. A few days later I got a call from Eddie Apex. He asked me to meet him at his place and to bring along a representative piece from the collection. So I brought along my father's favorite. Have you ever been to Eddie's house?"

"Yes."

"Isn't it weird?"

"Yes," I said, "isn't it. What happened then?"

"Well, not much, really. Eddie just looked at the sword for a long time. I mean he simply held it and looked at it without saying a word. Then he asked if he could keep it for a couple of days. I said of course and he wrote me out a receipt. Three days later he called and asked if he could give me lunch, that he had some rather important and exciting news. Well, we met at his club and after he had got a couple of whiskies into me he told me what the sword actually was and that it might be worth anywhere from one million to three million pounds."

"How did you feel?"

Robin Styles leaned back in his chair and stared at Mr. Hilton's ceiling. "You know," he said in a thoughtful tone, "I remember exactly. I think I had about three bob in my pocket and a hundred pound overdraft at my bank. I remember getting this feeling of tremendous sexual excitement. I simply had to have a woman. I didn't care what she looked like or who she was as long as she would fuck. And then I wanted a game. A real game. I wanted to get into bed with a woman and then I wanted to play poker. In that order." He looked at me. "Do you find that strange?"

"Uh-huh," I said. "But then nobody ever told me that I was suddenly worth a million or so pounds."

"Well, I decided to see if Eddie Apex were really serious. So I explained my financial condition and asked whether he could advance me some money. He said does this mean that you agree to let me and my colleagues handle the sword and I said of course. Well, he said, would five thousand pounds be enough and would it be all right if he sent it around later that afternoon in cash, because under the circumstances, cash would be better than a check. I nearly fell off my chair, of course. I was expecting something like three hundred pounds. But still that didn't satisfy my immediate needs. Sexual needs, I mean. So I said that would be fine, but could he spare fifty or a hundred quid now and he smiled and said, of course, and handed me over a hundred pounds. I went out that afternoon and got fucked most delightfully and does my crude way of speaking offend you?"

"Not in the least."

"Good. Well, a day or so later I met the Nitry brothers and aren't they the odd pair?"

"They are that," I said.

"Yes. Well, they gave me a little lecture on what the sword really was and congratulated me and told me that they had had it authenticated—I believe that was the word they used—by some chap in Maida Vale, of all places. They now intended to enter into negotiations for its sale. I said splendid and would it be possible to advance me a bit more money. They said Eddie would take care of that so Eddie and I came to an agreement. He would provide me with pocket money of a couple hundred pounds a week and guarantee my losses for up to fifty thousand pounds at Shields. I've very nearly reached that limit already."

"How long has it taken you?"

"Only a couple of weeks."

"And then the sword was stolen."

"That's right. The sword was stolen and I was shattered."

"I can imagine."

"I'm not sure that you really can, Mr. St. Ives."

I nodded. "Perhaps you're right."

"And you're going to get it back for us."

"I'm going to try."

He rose and stretched. His manners were too good to permit him a yawn. "Well, if you go about your calling the same way that you play poker, I feel that I'm in the best of hands. Thank you very much for breakfast, and now I think I'd better let you get some sleep."

"All right," I said, rising.

He paused at the door. "Eddie will be in touch with me when there're any developments, I suppose."

"Yes."

"Do you really think I could ever learn to play good poker?" From the wistful note in his voice, I knew that he wanted me to say yes.

"Maybe," I said. "At least there's one thing you have going for you."

"What?"

"A few million pounds. If you lose all that, you'll know for sure."

Chapter Thirteen

I was in bed by 5:45 that morning and probably asleep by 5:49 and the phone didn't ring until 6:01. I let it ring for a while on the theory that whoever was calling would give up or die, but when they didn't and since I never sleep too well with a phone ringing, I finally answered it with a snarling hello.

"We want the money this morning," the voice said. It was the same voice that had invited me down to the Black Thistle for Scotch and morphine. It was a man's voice and so neutral in tone and inflection that I couldn't tell whether he was American or English. He sounded as if he had acquired his accent in the middle of the Atlantic.

"I was asleep," I said, just to let him know that I tried to keep fairly decent hours.

"You're awake now. We want the money at seven sharp."

"That's less than an hour from now."

"And you're wasting time, aren't you?"

"I don't know whether I can get it."

"You can get it," the voice said.

"All right. Where?"

"Highgate Cemetery. Do you know it?"

"Ah, Jesus," I said.

"Do you know it?"

"I know it."

"All right. Here's what you do. Enter from Swain's Lane. Proceed to the statue of Marx and turn right. Do you have that?"

"Turn right at Marx," I said and thought about making some wise-ass remark, but decided that it was too early. Far too early.

"Proceed down the path until you come to the tombstone in the shape of an open grand piano. Time yourself so that you are there at seven o'clock sharp. I mean sharp."

I looked at my watch. "I've got six-oh-three," I said.

"It's six-oh-four," he said.

"Well, change yours."

That threw him a little, but not much. There was a pause and then he said, "All right, Mr. St. Ives, it is now six-oh-three."

"When I get to the tombstone that's shaped like an open grand piano, what happens?"

"The sword will be beneath the open lid," he said. "You will have two minutes to examine it. Then you will put the one hundred thousand pounds exactly where the sword was. You will be watched, of course. Then you will walk slowly back to the Swain's Lain entrance. I mean slowly. You will come alone. Do you understand?"

"I understand," I said, but I don't think he heard me because he had already hung up.

I immediately called Eddie Apex. It took him a while to answer the phone and when he did, he didn't sound overly chipper either. He growled something that sounded like hello, or who the hell is this, and after I told him, I said, "It's on and I need the money. Now."

That woke him up. "Where and when?"

"The switch is at Highgate Cemetery. I need both the money and transportation. I have to be there by seven."

When he didn't say anything for a moment, I said, "You're thinking."

"I've already thought," he said. "I'll send old Tom in the Rolls. He can pick up the money from Ned and Bert and drive you out to Highgate and bring you back. With the sword."

"With the sword. Have you got a hand magnifying glass? I never did pick one up."

"Bert'll have one."

"Tell him to give it to Tom."

"All right. What do you want the money in?"

"Anything that'll hold it."

"It's on its way."

My phone rang twenty-one minutes later which made it 6:28. I took a final swallow of the cold leftover coffee that I had warmed up with a large touch of Scotch. "It's Tom, sir," the old man's voice said. "I'm downstairs."

"I'll be right down," I said.

Old Tom looked as though he could have used a shave, but despite that he appeared spruce enough. He had on his uniform and cap and he held the rear door of the Rolls for me. Inside on the seat was a gray cloth bag, about the size of those once used by hotels for laundry. Printed across this one in faded gray letters was "The Roosevelt Hotel New Orleans."

"Where the hell did they get this?" I said.

He already had the Rolls in motion. "Bit of a panic there was, sir. It was all Mr. Norbert could find to hold the lolly."

I looked inside. There was a lot of lolly there, all in ten pound notes, some new, some old, and some in between, and all bound with brown paper wrappers that had £1,000 scrawled across them in pencil.

"They told you where to go?" I said.

"Highgate Cemetery, sir. Swain's Lane entrance."

"We have to be there by five till seven. Can we make it?"

Old Tom nodded. "Not to worry, sir. You just sit back and relax."

At a red light I dumped the money out on the seat and began counting the £1,000 packets. There were a hundred of them, just as there should have been. I always count the money. Carefully. The people I do business with take an exceedingly dim view of being shortchanged. In fact, most of them would be so upset that they might try to redress their grievances with various convincing arguments. A Louisville Slugger was one favorite.

I looked up. We were on Edgware Road heading north. The morning traffic had already begun to thicken, but most of it was headed the other way. Old Tom sat at the wheel of the Rolls, his arms straight out in front of him as if he were rounding an S-curve at the Nürburgring. I glanced at the speedometer. We were already hitting sixty.

"Might get a trifle bumpy, sir, from here on," he said, "so you'd best hold on to something."

I nodded and grabbed for the strap. Old Tom hit the brakes and drifted the Rolls around the corner and we were heading up St. John's Wood and by the time we flashed past Lord's we were going eighty.

We never went that fast again because from then on it was a series of side streets and back alleys and once the wrong way on a one-way street, which must have saved us seven seconds at least. The old man snapped the big car around tight corners as though he were driving a Porsche with beefed-up suspension. A Rolls is not supposed to be driven that way, but this one was, and it performed admirably. I decided that if any of my friends and acquaintances should ever be in need of a get-away machine, I could wholeheartedly recommend that they steal a Rolls-Royce.

As we careened around corners and raced down too-narrow streets, we collected our full measure of startled looks, honked horns, and rude curses. I clutched the strap, braced myself with my legs, and listened to old Tom as he whistled chorus after chorus of "Roll Me Over in the Clover." He whistled it off key.

Then we were through Highgate Village and heading

fast down Swain's Lane. Tom drew the Rolls smartly up to the curb, jumped out, opened my door, looked pointedly at his watch, and announced, "Three minutes till seven, Mr. St. Ives."

I didn't know whether he wanted a tip or a pat on the head. So I said, "You're damned good, aren't you, Tom?"

"I try, sir," he said, looking pleased.

"You're the best I've ever seen. You're even better than Cannonball Briscoe."

"Who's he, sir?"

"He drove for Pretty Boy Floyd," I said, making it all up. "After he got out of the slammer, he went on to make a name for himself in stock-car racing. Didn't you used to race?"

He nodded. "I once led Fangio for three laps, sir."

"That's something to tell your grandchildren about."

"I have, sir, and they don't really give a damn."

I entered Highgate Cemetery. My ex-wife, who was rather a weirdie in some respects, had discovered Highgate for me and when we had been flush enough, she would order the twenty-guinea picnic basket from Fortnum & Mason's, and we would lug it out to Highgate and spread our cloth under a tree and have our game pie and hock in the company of some angels who had had their heads knocked off.

I suppose that when you've been dead long enough they don't much bother with what your grave looks like at Highgate. The weeds grow up and the broken statues of various angels and saints and, for all I know, a few sinners tilt this way and that and sometimes fall down. The tall trees oversee it all and on a breezy day they seem to be gossiping about the foibles of the place's permanent guests.

One of those permanent guests is Karl Marx and his statue glares out at the hardy bands of pilgrims who journey to it from such places as Minsk and Ploesti and Sarajevo and, I suppose, Berkeley and Ojibway Falls. Even at seven o'clock there was a band of them there as I approached the tomb of the prophet. They wore big wide hot-looking suits and sensible dresses and they had scrubbed, Slavic faces and they were all taking each other's pictures. The one who nobody else would talk to, and there's one on every tour, shoved his camera at me and said something in a language that came from somewhere east of what used to be called the Iron Curtain. He was a prissy-looking type, with gold rimmed glasses, and rather than create an international incident, I put down the Roosevelt Hotel laundry bag and snapped his picture. Then he started gesturing and pointing and there was nothing to be done but for me to pick up my sack of £100,000 in Kapital and stand in front of the tomb of the old man who had taken such a dim view of it so that the tour outcast could take a picture of me and my money.

I turned right after the statue of Marx and headed down the graveled path. I remembered the tombstone that was carved to about a five-eighths scale in the shape of an open grand piano. I didn't remember who rested beneath it, but I long ago had made him up to have been a gay, insouciant type with a pleasant flat in Mayfair, an open Bentley, and any number of girls all called Pam and Jo and Liz who would plead with him to play something jolly as he entered the drawing room for drinks after having dressed for dinner. There's more to it, of course. With a cheerful nod and casual ease, much reminiscent of Fred Astaire, my dead hero would take his drink over to the piano and run through such numbers as "Beyond the Blue Horizon," "Nora," and "Avalon." This all took place, of course, in the spring of 1938 a few years after I was born. And he had died, this golden youth that my fantasy had placed beneath the open marble piano, during the Battle of Britain when his Spitfire bought it just after he had scored his fifth kill. He went down cleanly with no flames, of course, whistling "Nora."

During one of our picnics at Highgate I had made the mistake of telling my wife all this. She had looked it up and later informed me that no golden pre-war youth lay buried beneath the awful piano tomb. Rather it was a fat Armenian called Clarke who had changed his name from Keshishian. She had told me this, but I hadn't believed her.

There were more weeds growing up around the piano than there had been a dozen or so years ago when I had last seen it, but that was all right. The weeds in Highgate during the spring seem to take on a luxuriant green that would grace any garden.

I looked around but I could see no one, which didn't mean anything, because a full-strength platoon could have been hiding in the overgrown bushes or behind the tilting tombstones.

I approached the piano-shaped monument from the sloping side of its opened lid. I couldn't see any sword, but the lid could easily have been concealing it. I looked around once more, saw no one, made a dumb show of examining my watch, and when it was seven o'clock exactly I stepped up to the marble piano and looked beneath its open lid.

There was plenty of room for a three-or-four-foot sword. There was also plenty of room for the man who lay curled up there. I jumped, but he didn't move. He didn't move because his throat had been cut but there was no blood on the marble. His face was no longer pink. It was a pale, almost waxy white. His gray eyes were open and so was his mouth with its matching gray teeth. He still wore his gray tweed jacket with the black patches on the sleeves and on the crown of his head there was still the thick white scar that I had last seen when he had bent down to pick up the drink that he had knocked out of my hand at the Black Thistle.

There was no sword. I made sure of that. Then I backed away from the dead man. I backed away until I came to the path. Then I turned and ran all the way to the statue of Karl Marx and past that to the waiting Rolls-Royce.

Chapter Fourteen

*T*he crowd was big enough for a small wake and the gloom was thick enough for a huge one. Five of us were gathered in the red room of the Belgravia mansion on Groom Place: the Nitry brothers, Eddie Apex, his wife Ceil, and I. We were all slumped into various Victorian chairs and sofas, forming a rough circle around the Roosevelt Hotel laundry bag that squatted, a bit reproachfully, I thought, on the floor where I had dropped it.

Norbert Nitry sighed again, staring at the money bag. "So you think there's a mob of them, do you?"

He was looking at the money bag, but talking to me. I sipped some of the tea that I had chosen over coffee. It was quite good. "There were at least three to start with," I said. "Maybe four. Maybe even more."

"Why do you think so?" Ned Nitry said.

"Well, the dead man and whoever called me on the phone this morning weren't the same. I'd heard the dead man talk—in the Black Thistle that time—and he had a strong London accent. I don't think he could have changed his voice that much, but it really doesn't matter because by the time that I got the call this morning at six, his throat had already been cut and I'm assuming that he didn't make any phone calls after that."

They looked at me. None of them said anything. They simply looked at me as though daring me to go on and prove what I had said. I went on.

"When your throat's cut, you bleed, and usually you bleed a lot. It's messy. But there wasn't any blood around at the cemetery and that means he was killed someplace else and then taken to Highgate. Right?"

Nobody nodded. Nobody said damned good thinking there, St. Ives. They just looked at me until I answered my own question.

"Right. Now then, how do you get a body weighing around one hundred eighty or one hundred ninety pounds into Highgate Cemetery and tucked up underneath the lid of a marble piano?"

It wasn't exactly a rhetorical question, but I didn't get a nibble, not even a headshake. If I were going to ask damn fool questions, I was going to have to answer them, too, so I did.

"Well, you carry him," I said, "and if you're half smart, you carry him at night, and that means before dawn, which comes at about five-thirty this time of year and that means that the dead man was already dead and tucked away in his marble piano by the time I got my call this morning."

I would have settled for anything—even a polite sneer or a raised eyebrow. I got nothing, so I talked some more.

"Well, one man's not going to carry one hundred eighty pounds of deadweight. At least not that far. I know I couldn't. So he's going to have some help—at least one other person and possibly two. That means that there were at least three to begin with and now there're at least two, but possibly more."

I leaned back and waited. I don't know what I was

waiting for, possibly a *way to go, St. Ives!* What I got was a slow nod from Ned Nitry who said, "One hundred and eighty pounds. About thirteen stone, isn't it?"

"About that," I said.

Eddie Apex stretched his long legs out in front of him, folded his hands behind his head, stared at the ceiling, and said, "Why?"

"Why what?" I said.

"They could have had the money. We followed their instructions exactly. You were right on time. There weren't any police. What the Christ more do they want?"

"You asking me?" I said.

"You're the expert."

"Well, to use an expert's bromide, thieves fall out. The ones we're dealing with sure as hell have. Probably because a two-way split of a hundred thousand pounds is better than a three-way split. I still don't know how many are involved, but as I said there were at least three to begin with. And as for why the stall this morning, maybe they remembered who they're dealing with."

"What's that supposed to mean?" Apex said.

"He means, darling," Ceil Apex said, "that your reputation is still preceding you. You have been known to resort to the sly trick now and again. As for Dad and Uncle Bert, well, they're not usually thought of as being particularly angelic either."

"You think that's it, St. Ives?" Ned Nitry said.

I nodded. "Possibly. It could have been a combination warning and dry run. I've known some who've gone through four or five dry runs before they finally got their nerve up."

"I somehow don't think it's a question of nerve or their lack of it," Eddie Apex said.

"Not with a dead man with his throat cut, it isn't," Uncle Bert said. "Never did like slicers. Never did like doing business with 'em."

"We haven't got any choice though, have we?" his brother said.

113

"You think that's what it was, St. Ives?" Uncle Bert said. "That the dead bloke was sort of a fair warning?"

"I think they might have been trying to tell us something," I said.

"So what do we do now, wait?" Eddie Apex said.

I nodded again. "That's about all that you can do."

"What do you mean, 'you'?" Apex said.

"I don't like sliced throats and I like even less the people who go around doing it," I said.

Eddie Apex shot a glance at his father-in-law and then at Uncle Bert. If I hadn't been watching both carefully, I wouldn't have caught their almost imperceptible nods. "We'll go up to fifteen percent, Phil," Eddie Apex said. "Fifteen percent of one hundred thousand pounds. That's nearly thirty-six thousand bucks."

"I'm not trying to jack up my price."

"Of course not," Ceil Apex said. "It's just that Eddie's trying to provide you with a little incentive to carry on."

They were all staring at me now. I was the goose that was supposed to lay their golden egg and if I didn't, well, they could always have roast goose for dinner. I tried to decide who I'd rather have mad at me—the Nitry brothers or the sword thieves. I wasn't sure that it was much of a choice.

"All right," I said after a while. "One more time."

They all seemed to relax. I looked at my watch. It was a quarter past eight. I stood up. "I'm going back to the hotel," I said. "If they want to set it up again, they'll call me there."

"Anything else?" Ned Nitry said.

I looked at the laundry bag on the floor. "Yes," I said. "Find something not quite so cute to put the money in."

Even go-betweens must sleep, even the ones who play poker all night and stumble over dead bodies in the morning. I went back to the Hilton and went to bed and nothing at all happened until I awoke at a quarter till two that afternoon feeling hungry. I was New York-hungry, not

London-hungry, which gave me a couple of choices. I could either go to a place I knew off Leicester Square or I could try one of the Great American Disaster hamburger joints that had been touted to me by a couple of disenchanted tourists from Colorado Springs. Or I could be really adventurous and try a Wimpy Bar. I'd never eaten in a Wimpy Bar, but then I must be the sole remaining American who has never tried a McDonald's hamburger either.

A couple of reasons decided me on the place that I knew off Leicester Square and I decided to make a walk of it. I showered and shaved and dressed and then headed down Mount Street, because I happen to like it. I walked slowly, pausing now and then before the windows of the tony estate agent offices to admire photographs of some of the stately homes and country manor houses that I could steal for as little as a quarter of a million dollars.

I skirted the north end of Berkeley Square and paused on Bruton Street to gaze up at the window of the office I had once occupied. It had been nothing more than a partitioned cubicle really, but it had been a fancy enough address and at the time, that's what the paper thought I had needed. I hadn't really because I had written the column at home and had gone down to the office only for the mail and whatever gossip there was.

I went on, past the Westbury Hotel, down Bond Street, around Piccadilly Circus, over to Leicester Square, and down one of those small side streets that come out on Charing Cross Road. I wasn't sure that the place I had in mind would still be there, but it was, and the neon sign still read Manny's New York Delicatessen and Bar, Ltd.

The firm's managing director, principal shareholder, and chief bartender was Emanuel Kaplan, formerly of somewhere in the East End, Tel Aviv, Tangier, Marseille, San Francisco, and New York. After getting out of the British army in 1946, Manny Kaplan had led what has been described variously as an interesting life, a checkered career, and a villain's existence.

It is an establishable fact that he had helped Hank Greenspun run guns into Israel in 1948. It is equally provable that he smuggled cigarettes out of Tangier in 1949 and '50. Not so easily proved—or disproved—is his claim that he had spent the early fifties in San Francisco as constant companion to an aging sugar heiress who kept him on a five-hundred-dollar-a-week retainer. In the late fifties it gets a little murky although he was in New York and he did work in a Second Avenue bar and also in a Sixth Avenue delicatessen. When I had done a column on him more than ten years before, he insisted that he had acquired the capital necessary to open his present establishment by knocking over six savings and loan banks in Jersey. But when I checked it out none of the amounts and half of the dates of the robberies were wrong, although most of the details were right, so I decided that he probably had won his stake in a crap game and picked up the information about the robberies from the people that he palled around with in New York, who were some of the ones I knew, and who, for lack of a better description, could be called the wrong crowd.

When I walked into the place he was behind the bar and he hadn't changed much although he was close to fifty now. He still wore the perpetual cigarette in the right corner of his mouth and he was fatter and grayer, but who isn't. He looked up at me and said, "What the hell do you want, St. Ives?"

I sat down on a stool at the bar and said, "A corned beef on rye with a slice of onion and a bottle of Löwenbrau and, gosh, it's nice to see you, Manny."

"You know I don't handle no Nazi beer."

"Make it a Heineken if you're not mad at the Dutch."

Kaplan yelled my order at his sandwich man and served the beer himself. He spoke around his cigarette in a low, rapid tone that made almost everything he said sound private, perhaps even confidential, and he got his accent and his phrasing mixed up so that his speech was a curious blend of New Yorkese and Londonese, although neither was very far out of the gutter.

"I hear that you're in New York," he said. "I hear that you're back there and that you can't get a job and that you're doing something a little bent."

"Word gets around," I said and looked the place over. It hadn't changed. There was the long row of booths and some round stand-up tables and the bar and the refrigerated display case that was choked with all of the goodies that you'd find in any quality New York Jewish delicatessen. One wall was covered with autographed black and white photos of assorted actors, actresses, four playwrights, a couple of New York congressmen, three Members of Parliament, five bigtime gamblers, four pretty fair con men (including Eddie Apex), and about two dozen other photos of fox-faced men with wary eyes and strained smiles, a few of whom I recognized as being wanted by the police of at least two countries and possibly a third, if you counted Mexico.

I pointed at one of the con men. "I heard he got dropped in the bay at Hong Kong."

"He swum out," Kaplan said.

"Huh."

"How's your wife?"

"We split," I said.

"I wondered when she was going to wise up."

"How's business?"

"Terrible. I'm trying to work a deal with Nathan's, but they don't seem much interested."

"You think hot dogs would go over here?"

"How the hell should I know? McDonald's is moving in. Colonel Sanders and his goddamned fried chicken is already all over the place. Why not genuine Nathan's hot dogs? I could probably make a pile, except that Nathan's don't seem interested."

"I got an idea."

"What?"

"Real old-fashioned English fish and chips."

"Jesus, you're funny, St. Ives. You're really funny."

Kaplan took my corned beef on rye from the sandwich man and placed it in front of me. "One salt beef, sir."

He watched while I took a bite. Manny Kaplan had been handsome at forty, probably pretty at twenty, and now he was distinguished at fifty or so with thickly waving gray hair, a trimmed, gray mustache, a dark, brooding face with cynical black eyes, straight nose, and a box chin that was growing flabby.

"Well, how is it?" he said.

"It's fine."

"It's the best damned salt beef you'll find between here and Sixth Avenue."

I nodded at his stomach. "You look as if you've been at the potato pancakes again."

Kaplan looked down at his stomach that was half-covered with a long white apron that reached to his shoe tops. It was another New York touch. "What the hell," he said, "I'll be fifty-two next September." He looked at me. "You're as skinny as ever."

"I eat my own cooking."

Kaplan leaned his elbows on the bar and slipped on his most confidential look. "No kidding, Phil, what're you doing in town?"

"This and that," I said. "Last night a little gambling. Guess who I ran into?"

Kaplan ran through his mental list of our mutual acquaintances. I decided that it was a long one. "Probably in Mayfair, weren't you?" he said.

"That's right."

"Shields?"

"Uh-huh."

"Then you ran into Wes Cagle, didn't you? Now there's a right bastard."

"How long has Wes been in town?"

Kaplan thought about it. "A couple of years at least," he said. "How much did you lose?"

"I won a little."

"But you didn't come over to play poker, did you?" He picked up a bar rag and gave the old polished wood a couple of swipes that it didn't need. "You know, I keep up, I do. I hear it around that you're in a queer sort of business where you don't work too hard and where nobody gets too mad at you, not even the coppers, and you do all right for yourself, you do."

"That's what you hear, huh?"

"That's what I hear. So what I'm wondering is, is this. Is there any way you might want to cut me in?"

I shook my head. "Sorry, Manny. No way."

"So what the hell did you come down here for? Where you staying, the Hilton?"

"That's right."

"You would. You could've had 'em send you up a corned beef on rye."

"It's not the same."

"Sure it is," he said. "I supply 'em with a hundred pounds a week, although don't tell anybody I said so. You're not down here just for old times' sake. Our old times weren't that long or that good."

"I don't know about you, Manny, but I treasure those memories."

"Sure you do," he said, lighting another cigarette from the butt of the one that he took from his mouth. His hands would never touch the fresh one again until he used it to light yet another one.

"You interested in making ten pounds?" I said.

He looked up at the ceiling and spread his hands wide. "God, to think I should be reduced to this." Then he looked at me. "What do you want, a broad?"

"No, but I am looking for somebody. And it's worth ten pounds if I can find him."

He looked me over. "You're not suffering. Twenty."

"Fifteen."

"Done. Who you looking for?"

"Tick-Tock Tamil."

Kaplan's face broke into a large, white smile. "Jesus, I haven't even thought of Tick-Tock in years. I really mean in years."

"Is he still around?"

"How the hell should I know?"

"That's what I'm going to pay you the fifteen pounds for. To find out."

Through his arms that rested on the bar, Kaplan looked down at the floor, as though he might find the missing Tick-Tock's address written large at his feet. Then he looked up at me. "He was in the nick for a couple of years a while back, but I hear he got out. What do you want with Tick-Tock, a gold watch maybe that's just been stolen from the Maharaja of Rangpur?"

"Is he still working that?"

"Was the last I heard."

"Is he still into gold?"

If a man's ears can really prick up, Kaplan's did. "Be a good lad, Phil. If it's gold you're into, there's got to be enough to go around."

"I don't know what I'm into," I said. "That's why I want to talk to Tick-Tock. But if there is any way I can cut you in, I will. But don't bank on it. Anyway, there's fifteen pounds in it just for Tick-Tock's address."

"How the hell should I know where he lives?"

I sighed. "Make a phone call or two and find out."

Muttering something about snotty sonsofbitches who forget their old mates, Kaplan went through a door that must have led to his storeroom, whatever he used for an office, and the telephone. I looked at my watch, saw that it was five till three, and had the sandwich man bring me another beer before the law clamped down.

I was just finishing the beer when Kaplan came back. He had a piece of white paper in his hand. "Where's my fifteen quid?" he said.

I took out my wallet. "With the sandwich, two beers, and tip," he said, "that'll come to an even twenty."

I nodded at the stick-up and held out two ten-pound

notes. He took them and handed me the slip of paper which read, "13 Start Street, W.2."

"Where's Start Street?" I said.

"It's in Paddington. Where the hell else do you think Tick-Tock would live?"

Chapter Fifteen

I had been in no particular hurry to see Tick-Tock Tamil and I was back in my room at the Hilton, watching something about ants on BBC-2 and waiting for the phone to ring, when there was a knock on the door. It was a firm knock, even an authoritative one, and I wasn't especially surprised when my caller turned out to be William Deskins of Bunco and Fraud, or whatever Scotland Yard calls it.

"Twice in two days," I said. "Not quite enough to be called harassment."

I opened the door wider and he came in, wearing the same dark brown suit. He had on a different shirt though, a white one, and his tie looked something like scrambled eggs with chopped chives sprinkled over them.

"Do you mind?" he said, looking at the television set.

"Not at all. I was learning more about ants than I really wanted to know." I switched off the set.

"Over here," he said and moved over to the dresser. I followed him. "You ever gamble, Mr. St. Ives?"

"Now and again."

He took three playing cards from his pocket and dealt them face up on the dresser. The cards were the jack of hearts, the jack of spades, and the queen of hearts.

"Watch carefully," he said. "Keep your eye on the queen." He turned the cards face down and moved them about. His movements seemed to be neither tricky nor fast. "Now for five pounds, tell me which one's the queen."

"Let's make it for fifty," I said.

He moved the cards around some more, but this time his movements were a bit more flashy. "All right," he said. "For fifty."

"No bet."

"You know the game, do you?"

"Sure. It's a variation on the shell game, except that they make a production out of it here. There's usually a dealer, a couple of shills, and a lookout. They sucker you in and let you win a few times. Then they take you for everything you've got."

"There's a way to win though," he said.

"If you don't mind a broken jaw, there is. You can bet a couple of times and then try to walk off with your winnings, but I wouldn't advise it."

"Nor would I," Deskins said. He turned the cards face up and then face down. He moved them around a few times. "Where's the queen?" he said. "For gratis."

I tapped one of the cards. He turned it up. It was the jack of spades. "You're good," I said.

He turned all of the cards up, showing me the queen again, turned them face down, and started moving them around. I kept my eye on the one that I thought was the queen.

"Some of the lads had a little game going today in Shepherd Market just off Curzon. Know it?"

"I know it," I said and tapped a card. Deskins turned it up. It wasn't the queen. It was the jack of spades.

Deskins began moving the cards about again. "They

had a nice wood box set up, a couple of shills, and as you say, a lookout. They were working the luncheon crowd, you know."

"Uh-huh," I said. "That one," and tapped a card. It was the jack of hearts.

Deskins flipped the cards back over and began moving them around some more. "Who should come by but a busload of tourists."

"Well, Shepherd Market's pretty interesting. Sort of quaint. That one." I tapped a card and he flipped it face up. It was the jack of hearts again.

Deskins rubbed his hands together and started moving the cards around once more. "These were Bulgarian tourists," he said. "We don't get too many of those."

"That one," I said, tapping a card. He flipped it over. It wasn't the jack of hearts or the jack of spades. It was a photograph of me, the knave of nothing, standing in front of Karl Marx's tomb, holding a cloth sack that clearly read "Roosevelt Hotel," and wearing a silly smile that displayed most of my teeth.

"When you rubbed your hands together," I said.

"Mmm," Deskins said. "One of the Bulgarian chaps bet twice, won twice, and tried to walk away with his winnings. He's now in the hospital. Nothing broken, but possible internal injuries. He was still wearing his camera around his neck so we developed his film for him. You take a good picture, Mr. St. Ives."

"Oh, I don't know," I said. "I tend to freeze up."

Deskins turned from the dresser and crossed over to the window. He left the photograph of me where it was. "Nice view," he said.

"Pleasant," I said. "Especially this time of year."

He turned from the window. "Too bad about poor Billie Batts, wasn't it?"

"Was it?"

"They found poor Billie at Highgate about half past seven this morning, all curled up in a stone piano with his throat cut. Poor lad."

"You knew him?" I said.

"Yes. Didn't you?"

"No."

"Well, Mr. St. Ives, I did know him—in a professional way, one might say. That's why I'm here now, because I knew poor old Billie. But you say you didn't?"

"That's right. I didn't."

"Well, maybe you didn't know him by name, but only by sight. Take a look at this."

He crossed the room and laid another photograph on the dresser. It was a larger one, about five by seven inches, black and white, and it showed Billie Batts curled up underneath the open lid of the marble piano, wearing his tweed coat with the leather patches, his gray eyes open, his gray teeth showing, and his throat cut.

"You still say you didn't know him?"

"I didn't know him."

"I knew him for years," Deskins said. "He was always on the edge of things, poor Billie was. He pimped a bit, shilled when there was nothing better about, wanted to be a con man, but had neither the class nor the brains. He was too lazy to steal, Billie was, but got into porn in a small way for a while. He was a bust-up man for one of the protection rackets for a couple of years. Carried a razor, but I don't think he ever used it, except maybe once on one of his birds, but we could never prove it and she wouldn't talk. So really no one's too upset or even too surprised now that Billie's bought it."

"I didn't know him," I said, for lack of anything else to say. "I don't think I would have wanted to."

Deskins nodded, never taking his eyes from my face. "You play poker, don't you, Mr. St. Ives?"

"Sometimes."

"You've got a good poker face. I've been watching it. I can't tell whether you're lying or not."

I shrugged. A shrug is as good a way to lie as any.

"Well, as I said, they found poor old Billie Batts about

126

half past seven this morning. It was getting on for one before the Bulgar made his little mistake down at Shepherd Market. After the punch up and him landing in hospital, we developed his film on the chance that he might have taken some pictures of those who'd done the beating. You know how tourists are."

"Yes."

"Well, they brought the prints in to me and who should be standing there in front of Marx's tomb large as life but Mr. Philip St. Ives of New York. So I laid on a translator and we went to see the Bulgar. He was conscious by then. He said that you were a very kind gentleman who had just happened to be strolling down the path at Highgate Cemetery at seven this morning and who'd been willing to take his picture. And then he took yours, as sort of a souvenir."

"That's right," I said.

"And then, to the best of the Bulgar's recollection, you strolled on down the path—down toward where poor old Billie Batts lay dead with his throat cut. Is that right?"

"I went on down a path."

"What were you doing at Highgate at that time of morning, Mr. St. Ives?"

"My ex-wife and I used to picnic there," I said. "It was a long time ago. You might say I was making a sentimental journey."

"What was in the cloth sack?"

"My lunch."

Deskins sighed. "You know, Mr. St. Ives, I talked to the lads at the murder squad about you and we weren't at all sure whether I should come and see you or whether they should. They're not nearly as polite as I am."

"Most homicide cops aren't," I said.

"You've known a few, have you?"

"A few."

"Well, the lads at the murder squad had a preliminary report on Billie and it seems that he was done in about two o'clock this morning, give or take an hour or so. We decided we'd better find out where you were around that time."

"I was playing poker."

Deskins nodded. "At Shields. It seems that you won in one night more than I earn in a year."

"It hardly seems fair, does it?" I said.

"But you'll lose it back, won't you?"

"Next week," I said. "Or the week after. I stay about even."

"Yes," he said, running an appraising glance over me. "You haven't quite got what it takes to be a professional gambler."

"It takes hard work," I said and before he could think of something to say to that the phone rang. I answered it and the voice that I had last heard at six o'clock that morning said in its mid-Atlantic tone: "Are you alone?"

"No."

"Then just listen. You won't have to ask any questions."

"All right."

"Tomorrow morning buy yourself a pram. A large one."

"All right."

"I suggest Harrods. They have excellent ones there."

"All right."

"At three o'clock sharp enter the small church park that's just off South Audley Street between Mount Street and South Street. Do you know it?"

"Yes."

"I thought you might. Most Americans do. At three o'clock push your pram down to the section where it narrows and comes out on Carlos Place. There's a bench on the left. If you're in doubt about which bench, there's a small plaque on it that says that it's a gift from an American woman who spent many happy hours there. Do you understand?"

"Yes."

"Have the money in the pram. Sitting on the bench will be a young woman dressed as a nanny. She, too, will have a pram. In it will be the sword. You may bend over and inspect the sword for two minutes. She meanwhile will inspect the money in your pram. Is this all quite clear?"

"Yes."

"After two minutes, you will wheel the pram with the sword back up toward Audley Street. The girl will go in the opposite direction. Incidentally, dear man, do have the money in something a trifle more convenient this time, will you?"

"Yes."

"As for trying something clever, such as taking a picture of the girl, or finding out who she is, don't bother. She will be hired for the afternoon and she will know absolutely nothing. Oh. One more thing. You will be watched, of course. Now is everything quite clear?"

"Yes."

"Good," said the man on the phone and hung up.

I put down the phone and turned back toward Deskins. "Three all rights, one no, and five yeses," he said. "Your telephone conversations aren't too informative, are they?"

"I hadn't thought about it."

He stared at me for a long moment and then said, "Eddie Apex."

"What about him?"

"You're up to something with Eddie, something that smells, but I don't know what."

"Why don't you ask Eddie?"

"I already have. This afternoon. I asked him about you and I asked him about poor Billie Batts."

"What did he say?"

"He said you were an old and good friend of his."

"What's he say about Batts?"

"He said he'd never heard of him and you know what I thought?"

"What?"

"I thought he was lying both times."

Chapter
Sixteen

The cab driver didn't like Tick-Tock Tamil's address on Start Street in Paddington and he didn't think that I should either.

"You sure you got the right address, sir?"

"I'm sure," I said, handing over what was on the meter plus an adequate tip.

He shook his head. "I wouldn't go in there, not if they paid me."

"That's because you've got good sense," I said, but he was already driving off.

I suspected that the house at 13 Start Street had never been much of an address, not even when it had been built eighty or ninety years before. It had always been ugly, this cramped three-story structure that was far too narrow and built of dark and dirty brick that made it virtually indistinguishable from the rows of houses that had been thrown up on both sides of it.

What did distinguish 13 Start Street from its neighbors was that not all of its windows were broken out, or boarded up, as were the ones in the rest of the houses that lined the street. Across the way, old posters covered the vacant fronts of three shops that had once housed a dry cleaner, a butcher, and a tobacconist.

It looked like a condemned street, condemned by time and decay, or perhaps by speculators, or even by the ruling local politicians who may have decided that they should substitute another square mile of gloomy council flats for another square mile of gloomy slum dwellings. Everyone else on the street had moved, or fled, except Tick-Tock Tamil who appeared to be the lone holdout. I assumed that he was exercising squatter's rights at 13 Start Street and that whoever owned the building was having one hell of a time getting him out. I understand that if you know the ropes, you can do that in London— squat. Tick-Tock would certainly know the ropes.

There was a bay window and to the right of it a short flight of steps. I went up the steps and knocked on the door. The bay window had curtains whose pattern of faded red and yellow roses was turned toward the street so that passersby could admire the occupant's good taste. The curtain moved a little as someone peeked out. After a few moments a young blond girl, not much more than seventeen or eighteen, opened the door and let me look through her see-through blouse.

"Hello, love," she said. "Like to come to our party?"

The blond hair had come out of a bottle or a tube, but she seemed to have spent a lot of time on it, and it hung down in carefully careless ringlets. Her face was pretty in a pinched sort of way, but she wore too much makeup, especially too much green eyeshadow. She took a deep breath so that I could have a better view of what lay beneath the see-through blouse. What there was, was fine.

"Tick-Tock in?" I said.

"I'm sure I don't know who you mean."

"Mr. Tamil," I said.

"You a friend of his?"

"Of long standing."

"You're not the law."

"No."

"You know why I know you're not the law?"

"No. Why?"

"Because you're American, ain't you?" The "ain't you" came out more like "einchew" and the rest of her words had a strong London tang. She was, I decided, a native daughter.

"Why don't you be a good girl and run tell Tick-Tock that I'd like to see him."

She shrugged and turned her head. "Tick-Tock!" she screamed.

"What?" It was a man's voice.

"There's a Yank here who says he's a friend of yours."

He had changed. The last time I had seen him had been in the Ritz Bar and he had been wearing white tie and tails. It was one of his work uniforms then. On his head had been a white silk turban and in his pocket was a large, old-fashioned-looking watch, heavy enough to be made out of solid gold. Its back flipped open and there, in what appeared to be fine engraving, was inscribed, "To His Most Royal Highness from his Most Loyal Friend." And underneath that was the single name: Curzon.

"I move nearly a dozen of them a week," Tick-Tock had told me as we had sat there drinking our whiskies under the Ritz Bar's swooping pink and cream ceiling. "They bring anywhere from twenty to fifty pounds each —the average is about thirty-five."

"What do they cost you?" I had asked.

"Five pounds."

"They look to be worth a lot more."

"I have a chap in Hammersmith who runs them up for me. We use American insides and case. It's called a West-clox Railroad Special. We tried using Swiss works, but they don't tick quite loudly enough, if you follow me."

"Sure."

133

"Well, the engraving is not engraving at all. It's stamped, of course. The face looks hand-painted, but it's actually printed on special paper. And then we use a little lead here and there to give it weight."

"What about the gold?" I had said. "I'd swear that it was real gold."

"Oh, it is. But this chap in Hammersmith has his own method of electroplating. It spreads the gold so thin that if you just keep it in your pocket for a week or two, it will wear right through. I doubt that we use half an ounce on a hundred of them."

"How do you work it?"

"You will change my name, of course, when you write it?"

"That was the agreement."

"I really don't know why I'm doing this."

"Because you're going into something else," I had said.

"Yes. I suppose that's it. But you wish to know how I work it?"

"That's right."

"I work the older, better educated types, the ones who might recall or even care that Curzon was once viceroy of India—from 1899 to about 1905, I believe. Take that one over there—to your left."

I had looked to where an elderly type in a dinner jacket had been sitting for some time with a woman of about his own age.

"He'll be off to drop his penny in a moment," Tamil had said. "I suggest that you go first, sit yourself down, and then you can hear it all, even if you won't be able to see it."

"Okay," I had said and a few moments later I had found myself sitting on a toilet seat behind the closed door of a stall in the men's room of the Ritz Bar.

Tick-Tock had started the conversation in his impeccable accent. "I say, aren't you Sir John Forest?"

"No," I had heard the elderly gentleman say. "I'm afraid I'm not."

"Oh, I *am* sorry. There's such an extraordinary resemblance, but I suppose you're accustomed to it, being taken for him, I mean. I knew Sir John's son at school. You do know Sir John, don't you?"

"No. I don't know him."

"Extraordinary resemblance." There had been a pause and then Tick-Tock had said, "Oh, damn. I wonder if I'm running late? Do you have the time?"

"Quarter past nine."

Tick-Tock had chuckled. "Well, once more this old watch of mine is right and I'm wrong. But I don't really think that it's been more than a few seconds off since Lord Curzon gave it to Grandfather."

"Curzon?"

"Yes. When he was viceroy, you know. There's rather a touching inscription on the back, if you'd care to see it."

"Well, yes, I'd rather like that."

The elderly gentleman had read it out. " 'To his most royal highness from his most loyal friend. Curzon.' Well. Your grandfather, you say. Then you must be—"

Tick-Tock had interrupted. "Yes, I am, although I'm trying to be incognito, for tonight, at least. But this American reporter has tracked me down and I simply can't shake him. Perhaps you noticed him at the bar?"

"Can't say I did."

"Actually, the reason that I've gone to ground, so to speak, is not because of the American, but because of this blasted watch."

"Oh, really?"

"Yes. In point of fact, a chap from the British Museum has been after me night and day. They seem to want it most desperately and this chap was even so cheeky as to offer me a thousand pounds for the thing."

"A thousand pounds, eh?"

"I was tempted, if only to get rid of him. But I sent him packing, of course."

"Of course."

"Then there was this private collector who offered me five thousand for it. But he was Greek and you know what they're like."

"Damned rascals, most of them."

"Well, I must be going. This American reporter wants to do a story for his paper—*The New York Times*, I believe—on *my* London. It's, well, it's the London that you and I know, of course. Most Americans don't often see it."

"No," the old gentleman had said. "I doubt if they would. Or perhaps should." He had chuckled at his small joke and so had Tick-Tock.

"But I'm afraid that the chap from the British Museum is going to be on my trail tonight. He simply won't take no for an answer. He keeps telling me that the watch isn't really priceless, but I don't think that one can place price on sentiment, do you?"

"Of course not."

"I say, I have an idea. I know I'm going to put this wretchedly," Tick-Tock said, but he didn't. He had put it as smoothly as any proposition I've ever heard. It was his idea that the old gentleman should keep the watch for him, but only for the night. Tick-Tock would drop round to get it the next morning.

The old gentleman had protested, of course, but Tick-Tock had already thrust the watch upon him. When the old gentleman had made his final feeble protest, Tick-Tock struck. He had said that if it would make him feel more secure, the old gentleman could put up a pledge of perhaps fifty pounds. Caught between greed and flattery, the old gentleman had agreed.

There had been an exchange of names and addresses and telephone numbers and then they had made their good-byes. I had rejoined Tick-Tock in the bar shortly thereafter. The old gentleman and his wife had just been leaving. Tick-Tock had raised his glass in salute. The old gentleman had nodded and smiled, but a little nervously, I'd thought.

136

Tick-Tock had tossed me a small card on which a name, an address, and a telephone number were written. "He gave me a wrong address, a phony telephone number, and a phony name."

"How do you know?"

Tick-Tock had smiled at me and he had looked very much like Tyrone Power all made up to look like an Indian maharaja. "Because that's my business, mate," Tick-Tock had said. "To know."

Chapter
Seventeen

As I mentioned, Tick-Tock had changed in the more than ten years since I had last seen him. He didn't look like Tyrone Power anymore. He looked more like Gandhi.

"I know you," he said. "I remember you. You're Saint-something-or-other."

"St. Ives."

"Yes. St. Ives. What do you want?"

"Maybe he wants a party, Tick-Tock," the girl said.

"Shut up," he said. "What do you want?"

"Information."

He stared at me with dark eyes that had lost their flash and sparkle. All that remained in them was a kind of dead cunning. He had been not quite plump when I had last seen him, with quick and graceful movements, but now he was stick thin and when he moved, he jerked. He no longer wore a turban and what little hair he had left was egg-shell white and his dark skin, once smooth and supple, was dry and stretched with tiny deep wrinkles that gave him the tight, drawn look of a poorly done mummy. Tick-Tock was a mess and he was not quite forty.

"Information, is it? Well, come in."

We went into a sitting room that opened onto a primitive-looking kitchen. The sitting room was furnished with some old chairs and couches that seemed to have been rescued from a rescue mission. There was a four-color print of Jesus on one wall and in two of the chairs were sprawled two more young girls, one a blonde, the other a brunette. They both wore see-through blouses. The blonde wore a short skirt. The brunette wore pants. They smiled at me professionally.

"If you want one of these cunts, it's five quid for short time upstairs," Tick-Tock said in a mechanical tone. "Or you can have all three of them for a tenner."

"No thanks."

"Get out," he said to the girls. The two blondes and the brunette shrugged and left through the door that led to the kitchen.

"Want a drink?" he said.

"All right."

"Whisky?"

"With water."

"Whisky's seventy-five pence."

"All right."

He went over to a chest, took out a bottle of whisky, poured some into a smeared glass, and added water from a pitcher. He handed it to me. I gave him a pound. "Thanks very much," he said and made no move to give me the change.

"Want anything else?" he said.

"What have you got?"

He shrugged. "I've got hash and I've got pot. I've got cocaine. I'm fresh out of heroin."

I shook my head. "What the hell happened to you, Tick-Tock?" I said. "I thought you were into gold."

"What happened to me?" he said. "Two years in Dartmoor is what happened to me. And a cunt. God, I hate cunts. When was the last time I saw you?"

140

"Almost a dozen years ago."

"I remember now. It was in the Ritz, right?"

"Right."

"That was the night I quit the watch business."

"Yes."

"Well, the week after that my partner and I went to Paris and we spent almost every penny we had buying gold. We bought 1,280 ounces for forty-five thousand dollars U.S. A good price then. And we brought it back here with no trouble. No trouble at all. Then I went on a diet and lost two stone. It took me two months and I damn near starved, but I lost it. Then we had it all set. These two cunts and I would fly to Goa."

"With the gold," I said.

"That's right. With the gold. You know how much gold was bringing in Goa then?"

"No."

"Ninety-four dollars an ounce. Christ, it's more than that now, but do you know how much our profit would have been? Seventy thousand dollars. Net. For a plane trip."

"What happened?"

"My partner and I got greedy. We decided that since I'd lost so much weight, we could rig a special girdle so that I could carry fifty pounds with no problem. Originally I was going to carry forty pounds and the two cunts were to carry twenty each. But with me carrying fifty pounds, we only needed one cunt. She could carry thirty and look a little bit preggy, you know. It was what is known as an economy move. You want another drink?"

"You've watered the Scotch," I said.

"What did you expect?"

"Watered Scotch. I'll take another."

He fixed me another drink. "That'll be a pound," he said. I paid him.

"So what happened?" I said. "The girl you left behind blow the whistle on you?"

He nodded glumly. "She blew it all right. We barely stepped foot in Heathrow before they were swarming all over us. You asked what happened to me. Well, prison is what happened to me. Two years of it. Have you ever been in prison?"

"No," I said. "Not really."

"I couldn't stand it. I went crackers. I lost even more weight until I was nothing but skin and bones—just as I am now." He held out a thin arm for me to inspect. "My hair fell out. I developed ulcers. My teeth went. And when I got out after two years I looked just about as I do now and who would buy a gold watch from somebody who looked like me?"

"Nobody," I said.

"You're right. Nobody. So now I'm into brothel-keeping —on a small scale, of course. I push a few drugs, because if I didn't, I couldn't keep the cunts. I run an after-hours boozer with watered-down spirits and I sometimes peddle information for a fair price and what is it that you're after?"

"That partner of yours."

"Him!"

"You're still in touch?"

"Oh, yes, we're still in touch. After all, he's a fine Christian gentleman, he is. I went to prison and he did bugger-all. But every Christmas he comes around to see me with a big basket of treats."

"He faked those watches for you, didn't he? Could he fake anything else?"

"Him? He could fake the crown jewels if he put his hand to it. He's a bloody artist. What d'you have in mind?"

"Maybe a sword. Could he do an old sword?"

"No problem. He'd have to pray over it for a while, but he could do it. He takes his religion seriously. As I said, he's a proper Christian. After all, when I got out of the nick, didn't he set me up in this wonderful business I'm in? That's true Christian charity, isn't it?"

"You're bitter, Tick-Tock."

"You damned right I am."

"How much for his name and address?"

The dead cunning in his eyes moved over to let the greed in. "How'd you find me?"

"Manny Kaplan."

"Oh, him. What have you got on, St. Ives?"

"I don't know."

"Come off it. If you be needing an old Indian gentleman," he said with a quaver, "I could play me old grand-dad now instead of me."

"I don't think so, Tick-Tock."

"Just the name and address, right?"

"Right."

"Fifty pounds."

"Jesus."

"My ex-partner will be glad to introduce you to him." He pointed to the print of Christ on the wall. "He brought that around last Christmas. The cunts like it. Fifty pounds, please."

I counted him out fifty pounds. "His name's Billy Curnutt with a C and two t's and he lives over his shop at fourteen Beauclerc just off Hammersmith Grove."

"What kind of a shop?" I said.

"He's a locksmith when he's not down on his knees praying."

I rose. "Okay, Tick-Tock. Thank you very much."

"One more thing," he said.

"What?"

"He might be in low spirits."

"Why?"

"His wife left him this past Christmas Eve. I hear he's not over it yet."

"That's too bad."

"It's also something else."

"What?"

"It was the only good news I got last year."

Chapter
Eighteen

The Christmas tree tipped me off that something was wrong, which only demonstrates just how quick I am. If someone still has the Christmas tree up in the middle of May, fully decorated, although a bit brown, with the presents still lying beneath it, I tend to view it as unusual, even odd, although I had once kept mine up until the fifteenth of March.

I had had trouble finding a taxi and I hadn't arrived at the shop of William Curnutt, locksmith, at 14 Beauclerc Street until a quarter to six. Curnutt's shop had a big plate-glass window and behind the window was a drawn tan shade that had large white letters on it that spelled CLOSED. The locksmith's shop was nearly in the center of the block of small shops. Above the shops was a layer of flats. In the center of the block was a flight of stairs that seemed to lead up to the flats.

I went up the stairs and down a hall until I came to 14-B. I knocked, but nobody answered. I tried the door, more out of curiosity than anything else, since it was a locksmith's door, but it opened, so I went in.

The Christmas tree, a Scotch pine, I decided, was near a window. It was a big, fat tree, reaching nearly to the ceiling. Although the base of its trunk rested in a pail of water, there was a thick ring of brown needles on the mauve carpet and on the still unwrapped packages.

The furniture in the sitting room was neither good nor bad, just serviceable, sturdy stuff of no particular style that had been bought to last a long time and still had five or ten years to go. The lemon curtains were drawn, but two floor lamps were lit. On the walls were old mezzotints of Biblical scenes. David was about to do Goliath in with a slingshot. Adam and Eve were being driven out of the Garden of Eden by the stern forefinger of an old man with a long white beard who looked mad as hell. Some Roman soldiers rolled dice near a cross to which Christ was nailed. There were several others, all hardnosed, fundamentalist stuff, that seemed to hold out faint hope of there ever being a happy ending for the human race.

I went through the rest of the flat. There were two bedrooms, one of which must have been that of a child, a bath, a small dining room, and a kitchen. The beds were made, the bathroom looked scrubbed, and in the kitchen, which was almost fussily kept, things were laid out for tea.

The entire flat, except for the desiccated Christmas tree, which I took to be a sort of shrine, was almost too neat, as if it had just been cleaned by an overly conscientious daily, or as if its occupant couldn't abide a speck of disorder. There were no overflowing ashtrays; in fact, there were no ashtrays at all. No empty glasses or teacups. No ring around the bath. No bits of shaved beard in the basin. No unwashed dishes in the sink.

A flight of stairs led down from the kitchen, presumably to the shop beneath. I went down them and came out into a workshop that seemed to be even more tidy than the flat above. There was a place for everything and everything was in its place. Tools of all description were carefully set into wall clamps and brackets. Rows of nails, bolts, and screws were meticulously sorted and stored in capped,

146

labeled jars. A long, sturdy workbench with two big vises dominated one wall. Against another was a small industrial oven. There was also a gas-fed forge, some key-making machines, and several banks of blank keys.

In the center of the workshop was an old-fashioned blacksmith's anvil that must have weighed half a ton. Propped up against it was a man with a broken neck. He wore tan shoes and gray slacks and a white shirt. There was no tie. He was about fifty, I thought, although it was hard to tell because his head hung down at such an acute angle that his gray eyes seemed to peer up at me almost upside-down.

Although it was my second dead body of the day, I wasn't sure what I should do. So I stood there in the neat workshop and felt my palms grow slippery and the sweat gather in my armpits.

After a long moment, I made myself kneel down and touch his hand. For some reason then it was important that I touch him, as if it were the least that I could do for him, now that he was dead. The warmth had gone from his hand. It wasn't cold, but the warmth had gone from it.

I patted his rear pocket. There was a wallet in it. I took it out, opened it, and looked at the photograph of the woman who was too carefully posed with the five- or six-year-old child. The woman looked as though she were forty-five or forty-six, almost too old to be the mother of the child, a girl, but I somehow knew that she was and that she had left with the child on Christmas Eve and that now neither she nor her daughter would ever open the presents that lay waiting for them underneath the aging Christmas tree upstairs.

There were some cards of identification in the wallet that said that it belonged to William Wordsworth Curnutt, locksmith, who was fifty-one, and a resident of 14-B Beau-clerc Street, London, W.6. Other facts pertaining to the deceased included the information that he was a member of the Basic Baptist Breakfast Club, that he was male, five feet seven inches tall, weighed ten stone, had gray eyes, gray hair, no prominent scars, and that a gray suit was ready at the cleaners.

I put all the cards and scraps of paper and mementos that accumulate in a man's wallet back into the compartments that they had come from, after rubbing each one on my pants knee—to confound Scotland Yard, I suppose. Then, because I'm nosy, I opened the wallet lengthwise to find out how much money Billy Curnutt carried. There were four one-pound notes and the torn half of a playing card. It was the one-eyed jack of spades. It was poker size, rather than bridge size, but I thought that any kind of playing card would be a strange thing for a Basic Baptist to be carrying around, until I turned it over and saw the white letters that were reversed into its deep red front. The large letters spelled out SHIELDS and then in smaller letters underneath, A Gambling Emporium.

I stuffed the wallet back into the dead man's hip pocket and stood up holding the half card. I stood there, my back to the front of the shop, and I remember thinking that what I should do was to hurry with the card down to 221 Baker Street and knock up the principal resident there, tell him my tale, let him figure out what the card meant, and if he couldn't, perhaps he wouldn't mind giving his brother a ring.

That was the London I really wanted, of course, the London of clopping hansom cabs, and killing fog, and Sherlock Holmes, and bad drainage, mass poverty, a thirty-two-year life expectancy, and Queen Victoria.

What I had was London of the seventies with roaring inflation, a fading youth cult, a housing pinch, a Parliament that seemed to have lost its way, Queen Elizabeth, and a church-going Baptist forger with a touch of genius who preserved old Christmas trees and who lay dead at my feet of a broken neck at age fifty-one.

I like to think that I was lost in thought, but I'm afraid that it was fantasy again. Whatever it was, it kept me from hearing them. They must have been in the front of the shop, which was separated from the work area by a heavy tan curtain. I think I might have heard the curtain rustle. I sometimes still pretend that I did and that I carefully planned what followed.

But I don't think that I ever really heard them. I don't even think that I knew that they were there until they grabbed me from behind and slipped the cloth sack over my head. But I remembered what had happened the last time somebody had grabbed me from behind. I had used a couple of gutter tricks and I'd wound up in jail. I didn't use any gutter tricks this time, not even any pseudo-karate. I fainted. Or pretended to.

It wasn't easy, pretending to faint. I had to make my body go completely limp. The body doesn't want to do that because if it does, it's going to fall, and if it falls, it's going to hit something hard, and that's going to hurt. But I fell anyway and whoever had been holding me let me fall, out of surprise or out of hope that I would hurt myself and thus save them the trouble.

One of them said shit and the other one shhh. Then I heard them moving across the room. A door opened and closed. I took the cloth sack off my head and got up. Then somebody started pounding at the shop's street door. A voice yelled, "Mr. Curnutt! You in there?" It was a policeman's voice. I'm not sure how I knew that. I just know that I knew.

I didn't want to talk to any more policemen. Not just then. So I went the way that those who had grabbed me had gone. I went out the back door and down the alley. I didn't run. I wanted to, but I didn't run. And I didn't stop shaking until I was sitting in the bar at the very top of the Hilton with a double shot of I. W. Harper in front of me and another one already inside. I still don't know why I ordered bourbon. I really don't much like it.

Chapter Nineteen

*T*hey were pushing the roast beef at the Mirabelle that night, probably on the presumption that since I was American I would prefer hearty British fare to something French and funny. I ordered something French and funny anyhow, the blanquette of veal, because I wanted to see if they did it better than I did and, of course, they did.

Earlier at the Hilton I had called Eddie Apex and made what arrangements I had to for the next day. Then I settled down with the *Evening Standard* and read all about the Marble Piano Tomb Murder in Highgate Cemetery. It was the *Standard*'s kind of story and it had even pushed an old standby, GUARD DOG SAVAGES CHILD, back to page seven or eight. I read the dog story, too, only to learn that the child was a sixteen-year-old girl who had been teasing the dog who had nipped her. Once.

The *Standard* didn't have too many facts on the Highgate murder either, but it had gone with what it had. One William W. Batts, twenty-seven, of some place in Islington, had been found dead with his throat cut in Highgate

Cemetery, tucked up underneath the open lid of a marble grand piano. A mysterious Bulgarian tourist was helping police with their inquiries. That was about all they could dig up on the late Billie Batts, so they had turned to the other dead man, the one who lay buried beneath the piano, and I learned that my ex-wife had been right. He had been an Armenian and so there went another illusion.

I kept seeing Billie Batts's dead gray eyes and there was something about them that bothered me. So I telephoned the *Standard*, was given a sub-editor who sounded knowledgeable, and asked if he happened to know what the *W* in William W. Batts stood for.

"Why?" he said.

"Because a William Winston Batts owes me a lot of money," I said.

"I'll check," he said. After a few moments he came back on the line. "You're in luck," he said. "The dead chap in Highgate's name was William Wordsworth Batts."

I wanted to ask some more questions, but I had already asked one too many, so I hung up. I wanted to ask if the late William Wordsworth Batts's mother hadn't once been married to one William Wordsworth Curnutt, locksmith, and had divorced him years ago, taking her son with her. I wanted to ask whether she hadn't remarried and given her son the surname of her new husband. I wanted to ask those questions, but I didn't really need to because the still gray eyes of William Wordsworth Batts, ne'er-do-well, that had stared out at me from underneath the open lid of the marble piano had been just like those equally still gray eyes of William Wordsworth Curnutt, locksmith, that had stared up at me, sort of upside-down, as their owner had lain propped up against an old anvil, dead of a broken neck.

I sat there in the Mirabelle until ten, dawdling over coffee and wondering about the dead father and son and wondering, indeed, if they were father and son, and if they were, what they had been up to, and why were they now both dead. After three cups of awful coffee, I still didn't know, so I paid my bill, crossed the street, walked another hundred yards or so, and entered Shields, A Gambling Emporium.

Shields was a club, of course, as are all the gambling hells in London. At one time, tourists could join any of them for a pound or so. They still can, but they have to wait a while, forty-eight hours, I think, before they can lay their money down. I don't know who thought up this rule, or why, or even when, but I assume it was passed to give London's other fun purveyors a crack at the tourist dollar, or mark, or yen, before they fell to the croupier's rake.

William Deskins, the man from Bunco, didn't look much like a gambler or a tourist as he leaned against the bar, a glass of beer at his elbow. Instead, he looked like a cop who wanted to go home, but couldn't, because he had to wait for some idiot who was always late.

The man at the door said, "Good evening, Mr. St. Ives," and didn't bother to ask for any membership card, which I didn't have. I wasn't particularly flattered that the man remembered me. He should. He was the dealer that I had tipped twenty pounds.

"Cagle around?" I said.

"Yes, sir. Would you like to see him?"

"In a few minutes," I said and moved over to the bar.

"Hello, St. Ives," Deskins said. "I thought you might turn up."

"Ah, Inspector Deskins. What brings you out on a foul night like this?"

"I'm not an inspector and it's a nice night."

"It was just something that I've always wanted to say. I'll buy you a drink."

Deskins shook his head. "You're the odd one, you are, St. Ives. But I'll take your drink."

I ordered two large whiskies from the bartender and after Deskins had tasted his, he said, "Ever hear of a chap called William Wordsworth Curnutt?"

"Should I?"

"Perhaps. Somebody broke his neck for him this afternoon. Over in Hammersmith."

Deskins was staring at me over his drink. I decided not to say anything. There wasn't anything to say yet.

"Billie Batts, you remember, got his throat cut in Highgate this morning. Guess what Billie Batts's full name was."

"William Batts," I said.

"William *Wordsworth* Batts."

"You're trying to tell me, in your own wonderful way, that there's some connection between the two."

"They were father and son."

"Why the different surnames?"

"Billie Batts's old mum left Curnutt years ago when Billie was only a kid. She divorced him and married a chap called Batts. He legally adopted Billie and gave him his name."

"How long have you been waiting here?" I said.

Deskins shrugged. "Half an hour, perhaps."

"You haven't been waiting half an hour just to tell me this."

"You in a hurry?"

"I've got some money to win."

Deskins nodded. "You know where I've been earlier this evening?"

"Where?"

"Over in St. James's Square having a bit of a read."

I had to think about it. "The library's there," I said after a moment. "The London Library."

"It's hard on the eyes," Deskins said, and rubbed his as though to prove it.

"My column," I said. "You were reading my column. I'm flattered that you read it. I'm even more flattered that the library would have it."

Deskins nodded. "I read some of the ones you wrote while you were here in London."

"That was a long time ago."

"You had a nice light way of putting things."

"Thank you."

"But you wrote about some right bastards, didn't you?"

I nodded. "Mostly."

"Half of the ones you wrote about are inside now."

"I'm not surprised."

"The other half should be."

"Probably."

"You wrote a couple of columns that I liked especially."

"Oh? Which ones?"

"About Tick-Tock Tamil. You remember Tick-Tock?"

I nodded. "I remember him."

Deskins smiled at me over his drink. "Old Tick-Tock could flog a gold watch if anyone could. But you know something?"

"What?"

"We never got a complaint. Not one. Tick-Tock was a clever bastard, he was. He never really sold them, you know. He made his victims think that they were stealing them from him and when they found out that they'd been had, well, they were too ashamed to do anything about it. But you wrote all that, didn't you, except that you changed Tick-Tock's name."

"That was the deal."

"The only thing you didn't write about was Tick-Tock's partner, the chap who supplied him with the watches."

"Tick-Tock wouldn't tell me who he was."

"His name was William Wordsworth Curnutt. Billy Curnutt. Locksmith. Family man. Forger. Churchgoer. Father of the late Billie Batts and dead himself of a broken neck at fifty-one."

"Well, you've had a busy day, haven't you?"

"After I left the library, I began thinking about it. I got to thinking that there's something that connects you with it all, St. Ives. You were out at Highgate this morning where Billie Batts got his. You once wrote a column or two about Tick-Tock Tamil who was once the partner of Billie Batts's old dad—who'd just died of a broken neck. And then there's Eddie Apex and the Nitry brothers and God knows what you're seeing them about. But somehow, it's all connected, isn't it?"

"I don't see how," I said.

"Well, I couldn't either so after I left the library I decided to drop round and see Tick-Tock to find out whether he might know something. Tick-Tock lives in Paddington, you know."

"Does he?"

"He's always lived in Paddington. He was born there. For the past six months he's been living someplace where he shouldn't and they've been trying to get him out, but he's got the law on his side, so there he stays and pays damn all rent. So I thought I'd drop round and chat him up a bit. But guess what I found?"

"What?"

"No Tick-Tock. He'd cleared out."

"Just when you needed him."

"That's right. Just when I needed him."

"That's too bad."

"Oh, not really. I've got another good lead."

"What?"

Deskins put his glass down on the bar. "I've got you, St. Ives, and I've also got the feeling that you're all I'm going to need. Thank you very much for the drink."

Chapter
Twenty

*T*he twit dealt. That's how I still thought of Robin Styles, the overly elegant young man who just might possibly be worth a few million pounds or so within the next few days or weeks, providing I got his sword back for him.

He had wanted to play, of course, but he had exhausted his credit earlier in the evening and neither Wes Cagle nor I would accept his marker so we let him deal the head-to-head stud game that we were playing in Cagle's fancy office. We were playing no limit, raise-when-you-want-to poker, and we had been playing for three hours and I was nearly a thousand pounds down.

Five-card stud, when played by two persons, is often dull, relentless gambling, even when played for very high stakes. You tend to get overly reckless or overly cautious, neither of which makes for good poker. I had been too reckless earlier in the night and now I caught myself overcompensating by playing too carefully.

Cagle played like a machine, a huge six-foot-seven, 275-pound machine, some of it fat, that loomed over the green baize of the round Victorian table, dwarfing both Robin Styles and me. Cagle rode his luck when he had any. He rode it hard, too hard perhaps, and I kept waiting for the hand that he would have to ride because his skill and his luck and everything that made him a gambler would tell him that this was the hand that both of us had been waiting for all night—the hand that would bust one of us.

It was a pleasure to watch Robin Styles deal. He seemed to go with the elegant room that was Wes Cagle's office. It was Victorian, but gracefully so, with the best that age had had to offer. Whoever had decorated it had known that mauve can be a pleasing shade, if it's done right, and Cagle's office was done right. He had the only inlaid roll-top desk that I had ever seen and there were chairs and a couch that curved elegantly and looked comfortable. The bric-a-brac was just that, bric-a-brac, but it went with everything else and I thought that the decorator had succeeded in accomplishing what he had set out to do: create a room in which vice might flourish. All kinds of vice.

Cagle and I were down to our shirt sleeves, but Robin Styles sat there, and dealt, looking well pressed and unrumpled, his jacket still on, but his tie loosened an inch or two to signal that he was feeling at least part of the strain. If he had fixed his tie, he would have looked as if he were all set to drop by for a noon drink at his club. Probably Guards.

He dealt effortlessly and as prettily as anyone I have ever seen. The cards flowed from his fingers, landing exactly where he wanted them to. He probably did everything well with that same effortless grace, except the one thing that he wanted to do well more than anything else. Gamble. He still gambled like a twit.

He had just dealt me the two and four of hearts. The four was my hole card. Cagle had a king showing. He bet a hundred pounds on it so I assumed that he had paired it. I called. My next card was the ace of hearts. Cagle got a jack of diamonds. Robin Styles called my hand for what it was, a possible flush. I checked to Cagle who bet another hundred. I called.

My next card was the five of hearts. Cagle was dealt another king, which gave him two up, and probably one in the hole. He bet them that way anyhow. He bet five hundred pounds.

I had a four-card flush. I ran through the odds of my landing another heart. I decided that it was worth it so I saw Cagle's five hundred pound bet.

Robin Styles knocked the table and said, "Set?"

"Cards," Cagle said.

Styles dealt Cagle the one-eyed jack of spades. Cagle couldn't keep the glint out of his eyes. I didn't blame him. He had a pair of jacks and a pair of kings showing, and probably another king in the hole. He had a full house.

Styles dealt me the trey of hearts and it stopped my heart for a second. I had the ace, deuce, trey, and five of hearts showing. In the hole I had the four of hearts. I fought back the almost overwhelming temptation to peek at it, to make sure that it was really there. But I knew it was there and I knew that I had a low straight flush and that it would beat any full house ever dealt.

I could almost sense Cagle's mind running through the odds to see what they were against my having the four of hearts in the hole. They were astronomical. He could beat a flush with his full house. But he also knew that I would call him: that I would virtually have to call him, if I had my flush.

"Well," he said, "what have we got here?"

"You've got two pair showing," I said. "You bet."

"So I do," he said. "I shall bet one thousand pounds." He shoved his chips in. They lay there and glowed a little, the way one thousand pounds will do.

I had my hands in my lap. They wanted to shake, so that's why I had them there. "Up a thousand," I said and used one of my hands, the least shaky one, the right, to push two thousand pounds' worth of chips into the center of the table.

"Well," Cagle said. "That do make it interesting."

"You know something, Wes?" I said.

"What?"

"You don't much talk like a Princeton man."

"Fuck off."

"See what I mean?"

"I'll see your raise and bump you a thousand, St. Ives," he said and pushed the chips into the center. I looked at the pile of chips. There should have been £6,400 there—nearly $16,000, depending on what the dollar was doing that day. It was a big pot. It was, in fact, the biggest pot I had ever been in on. I wondered whose money Cagle was playing with—his or the house. I knew whose money I was playing with—the installment loan department's at Chase Manhattan.

"Up two thousand," I said, "and I'll have to write you a check."

I think it was about then that Cagle got the message. "You son of a bitch," he said and watched while I took a blank check from my wallet. My hands were better because I no longer cared whether he saw them shake. I wrote the check out and tossed it onto the pile of chips. Cagle shoved in the stack that would cover my raise.

"You're just calling," I said.

"I'm just calling."

I turned my four of hearts over. "Straight flush," I said.

Robin Styles gasped and Cagle's lips moved as he silently counted up to five to make sure that I wasn't lying. Then he turned to Styles and said, "Deal," as I raked in the chips.

"I'm cashing in," I said.

Cagle made no protest. Maybe he had learned his good manners at Princeton, although maybe they weren't good manners at all, but good business practices that he had learned in Vegas. I started counting out the chips and Cagle counted with me. Robin Styles watched fascinated and I remember thinking that I had probably ruined him for life. It had been the big hand that all gamblers dream of and now that he had seen it come true, he would pursue his own vision of it forever, no matter how far down it might lead him.

When I was through counting the chips, I took something else from my wallet and flipped it at Cagle. "How about this, Wes? How much is this worth to you?"

It was the torn half of a one-eyed jack of spades that I had removed earlier from the wallet of William Wordsworth Curnutt of the broken neck. I watched Cagle carefully as he picked up the torn card, looked at the face of the knave, and then turned it over as if to see what was written on the back. The only thing written there was the reversed letters that spelled out SHIELDS, A Gambling Emporium, but they were supposed to be there, and Cagle flipped the half card back to me along with a disgusted look.

"Are you trying to be funny or something?"

"I don't guess it was a very good joke," I said.

"No it wasn't. At least I didn't understand it. Did you understand it, Styles?"

Robin Styles moved the knot in his tie up until it was firmly mounted in his collar. "Well, no, I don't think I really understood it either," he said.

Wes Cagle rose and stretched. He looked huge doing it. But then he was huge. "How do you want it, St. Ives, pennies, nickels, or dimes?"

"Any way at all," I said.

Cagle nodded and moved over to the wall, swung back a painting, and started dialing the numbers of a combination safe. He looked bored, so I decided that it wasn't his money he had been playing with. He counted out eight thick stacks of ten pound notes. "Eight thousand," he said. He counted another smaller stack out. "Plus four hundred. Right?"

"Right," I said.

"Close to twenty thousand bucks. Not bad."

"Not bad," I agreed.

"We even give you a doggy-bag to take it all home in," Cagle said and put the money into a shiny black plastic bag with a zipper opening. He handed it to me. "We'll try it again sometime," he said.

"Soon," I said, lying as well as I could. I turned to

Robin Styles. "Come on," I said. "You can ride shotgun."

"What? Oh, yes, I see. Of course."

"I'll get you a cab," Cagle said.

"Thanks."

I turned and headed for the door, Robin Styles close behind.

"One more thing, St. Ives," Cagle called after me.

I didn't stop. "What?" I said over my shoulder.

"Remember where you won it, and tell your friends. If you've got any."

Chapter
Twenty-One

*T*he invitation to breakfast at Robin Styles's was issued so politely and hesitantly and with such diffidence that I couldn't bring myself to turn it down. But first I had the cab stop by the Hilton where I handed what I had won over to the desk for safekeeping.

It wasn't far to Styles's place. It was just north of Bayswater Road near Lancaster Gate. As I paid off the cab, Styles stood looking up at the three-story building. "A bed-sitter in Bayswater," he said. "Some friends of mine knew a chap who killed himself because he was afraid he would end up like this."

"When you get all that money you can move out to Hampstead where you belong," I said.

We went up two flights of stairs to the bed-sitter that was home to Robin Styles. I couldn't help comparing it to my own "deluxe" efficiency in the Adelphi. It was with a sense of shamed relief that I decided that mine was far better. But that was because along the way an architect had had something to do with its original design. And, too, I lived where I did out of a kind of perverse choice, while Styles lived where he did because he had to and because he was one of those persons who are just basically unlucky.

It had been a bedroom in a large townhouse at one time and even then it must have been small, good enough perhaps for the upstairs maid, but certainly not for nanny.

It was about nine by twelve feet and it had one window. There had been a closet, but it was now the bath although if you sat down on the toilet you had to sort of slide onto it and then the washbasin was in your lap. The kitchen was in one corner of the room and consisted of a wooden chest that held a two-burner gas stove that was not quite a hotplate. The refrigerator was a three-foot-high Frigidaire, the 1936 model, I thought, that might have brought a few dollars in New York as a campy sort of antique.

The furniture was not quite bad enough to be awful, but almost. There was a single bed that doubled as a sofa, a couple of straight-backed wooden chairs, an "easy" chair that looked anything but that, a bridge table that seemed to be serving as desk, dining table, and a place to practice poker hands, a gray rug, and a large old armoire that must have held Styles's wardrobe.

Styles didn't apologize. He only said, "It was about what you expected, wasn't it?"

"You're very neat, aren't you?" I said, which was the only thing I could say that came close to being nice.

"Habit," he said and opened the wooden chest that supported the two-burner stove, took out a bottle of Scotch, and poured two drinks into glasses that I suspected had once held jam. Or maybe marmalade. He ran some water from the bathroom basin tap into the glasses and handed me one. "Sorry, but I don't bother with ice because the Fridge only makes six small blocks."

"That's okay," I said.

Although I didn't time him, I think it took no more than four minutes, and possibly less, for Robin Styles to serve up one of the best omelets I have ever had. He moved like a skilled chef in that corner that was his kitchen. He broke four eggs into a bowl, using only one hand to do it, a trick that I've never been able to master. While he was beating them, he had a large copper omelet pan, possibly the best piece of furniture in the place, heating on one of the burners. When the pan was hot, he dropped in a chunk of butter and went back to beating his eggs with a wire whisk, stopping only to dump in a pinch of this and a pinch of that from some containers that looked suspiciously like old cold cream jars.

The eggs and the butter were ready at the same time, something else I've never been able to arrange, and he poured the eggs in and then began moving the pan back and forth over the flame while using a rubber spatula to stir the top portion of the eggs so that they would cook properly. It was a little like rubbing your stomach and patting the top of your head at the same time—far harder to do than it looks.

In less than a minute, and probably closer to thirty seconds, he removed two plates that had been warming, set them on the card table, brought the pan over, gave it a sharp rap with a knife, and I watched the omelet fold over perfectly. Then we sat down and had Scotch and possibly the world's best omelet for breakfast. Or late supper.

"You do a lot of things well, don't you?" I said.

"Not really."

"Do you ride?"

"I once did, but I had to give it up. Too expensive, you know. There was a little talk about my entering international competition, but it was only that. Talk. I also shoot and I once went in for a bit of amateur sports-car racing; I've sold a few paintings and even some rather stylish photographs. I've written a few reviews for *The Observer*. And I play the piano a little like Duchin and poker like a guppy."

I leaned back in the wooden chair and lit a cigarette.

"You could really enjoy it, couldn't you?" I said. "Being rich, I mean."

"Oh, yes. Definitely. There are any number of splendidly expensive things that I have done and could still do, if I had the money. Although I do all of these other things rather well, I just can't gamble. I don't know why, but the more badly I play, the more I must. Simply must."

"I've known some who've quit," I said. "Compulsive gamblers."

"Not ahead?"

"No, not ahead. They'd lost it all."

"How were they? After they'd quit, I mean."

I thought about it. "Paler, I suppose. And quieter. Much quieter. It seemed as if they were listening for something."

Styles was silent for a moment. Then he said, "I thought it was all going to be so simple. I mean after they told me what the sword really was. I thought I was going to be enormously rich and that I would put most of it away somewhere so that I couldn't touch it and live off the income. Live jolly well, too."

"Maybe you still can," I said.

He shook his head. "I don't know. It's all grown so damned complicated. Tonight, for example."

"Tonight was simple," I said. "I won a lot of money. Wes Cagle lost a lot. You dealt."

"Not that. It was when you showed him that half of a playing card. I didn't think I should say anything then. I'm not sure why, but—" His voice trailed off.

"But what?" I said.

"Well, this," he said. He brought out his wallet and flipped something onto the table. It was half of a playing card, half of a one-eyed jack of spades. He watched as I reached into my own wallet, took out the half I had, the half that I had lifted from the wallet of the dead Billy Curnutt, locksmith, and moved it across the table until its torn edge reached the other half. They fitted perfectly.

"Where'd you get yours?" I said.

Styles looked uncomfortable. "I'm not really sure that I should tell you."

"You'd better," I said, "or Eddie Apex is going to be looking for a new go-between."

"I don't understand it really," he said. "You see, this torn card was given to me just after I was first approached by Apex and the Nitrys. It was just a few days after that, before the sword had even been stolen. I was flushed with how rich I was going to be, so I really didn't think much of it. I suspect that I thought that it was all part of the romance and intrigue that seemed to envelop the entire thing."

"Who gave it to you?" I said.

"It was given to me one afternoon—when we were alone. And the person who gave it to me said that if anything ever happened and the deal for the sword didn't come off, and somebody simply tried to hand me back the sword and advised me to go peddle it somewhere else, through legal channels, I suppose, I was not to do so. Not unless the matching half of this card was presented to me along with the sword." He paused. "It was all—well, so melodramatic that I really didn't pay much attention. But now you have the missing half. And I don't understand."

"Who gave you the torn jack?" I said.

He bit his lip and I don't think he was much of a lip biter. "Well, it was Ceil. Ceil Apex. Eddie's wife."

"She was the one then, wasn't she?" I said. "The woman that you had to have that afternoon that Eddie Apex told you how rich you were going to be. It wasn't a whore. It was Eddie Apex's wife. That must have added a touch of titillation."

"It wasn't that way. I've known Ceil for years. I knew her before she ever met Apex. We were very close, in fact, at one time. Very close, and then we just drifted apart—the way it happens. Then when we met at Apex's, we both knew it was going to happen again. At least once, anyway. And when it did, she gave me the torn card and told me

167

just what I've told you. But from the look on your face, I don't think you believe me."

"That's just another one of the reasons that you shouldn't play poker," I said.

"Then you believe me?"

"Yes, I believe you."

"Well, I'm afraid I don't understand."

I took my half of the jack and put it back in my wallet. "I'm going to give you some advice. You do exactly what Ceil Apex told you to do."

"You mean I shouldn't accept the sword if they try to turn it back to me?"

"Not unless the other half of that jack of spades goes with it."

"But you've got the other half."

"That's what I mean," I said.

Chapter
Twenty-Two

The ringing phone awoke me at eleven o'clock that morning and on the other end was the aged Apex butler, Jack, once known as Gentleman Jack Brooks, notorious jewel thief and scourge of the Riviera.

"The pram cost fifty-two quid, sir," the ex-scourge said.

"You must have bought the best."

"Bottom of the luxury line at Harrods. That's always the best buy, sir."

"You downstairs?"

"Yes, sir."

"You have everything else?"

"It's all tucked into the pram."

"Well, you'd better come on up."

"Right away, sir."

The tea and toast that I ordered beat Jack to my room. I was just pouring a cup when he knocked at the door and wheeled in what may have been the fanciest baby buggy in London. It was a glistening black with a convertible top, big wire wheels with white rubber tires, and little round clear plastic windows so that its small occupant could look out at the trees when the top was up.

Old Jack seemed proud of his selection so I said, "Very nice. Very nice indeed. Did they throw in a tape deck?"

"Beg pardon, sir?"

"Why don't you have some tea while I count the money?"

"Thank you, sir. I wouldn't mind a cup."

This time the money was in a large attaché case that was tucked up all nice and warm under a pale blue blanket. I took the case over to the top of the TV set, opened it, and counted the money. It was all there so I tucked it back up in the pram.

"Everything all right, sir?"

"It's fine. Thanks very much, Jack."

"Oh. One more thing, sir. Mr. Ned asked me to give you this."

He reached into his pocket and brought out a large, round magnifying glass. "You forgot it the last time out," he said.

"So I did." I took the glass and slipped it into my bathrobe pocket.

"I was just thinking, sir, on the way over from Harrods. I could have used a gentleman in your line of work once. Old Tom and I were talking about it the way a couple of old lags will; no offense, sir."

"I'm flattered. You were one of the best. They never did tag you to that New Weston job you pulled in twenty-nine, did they?"

The old man stiffened and then relaxed. Then he smiled and I decided that he must have had a lot of charm and style at one time. "There's only one person that could have told you about that, sir."

I nodded. "Sammy Farro. I spent a couple of days with him after he got out of Dannemora in sixty-three."

"I didn't even know he was inside. Old Sammy."

"He killed a man on Park Avenue in thirty-two. There was an emerald necklace that Sammy had his eye on. The man and his wife came home early, the man pulled a gun, there was a fight for it, and the man got shot. Danny got life. He did thirty years."

"The New Weston Hotel," the old man said in a dreamy tone. "We made a proper haul that night."

"They tore it down," I said.

"How'd he look when he got out?"

"Bad," I said. "His mind was going, but he remembered you. He said some nice things about you."

"Oh, he was a smooth one, Sammy was. Is he still about?"

"He died a year after he got out," I said. "Alone in a room. They didn't find him for a week."

The old man put his tea down and rose. "Too bad you weren't around back then, sir. We might have done some business."

"We might have at that," I said.

After Gentleman Jack Brooks left, I had room service bring up a typewriter. I sat before it in my bathrobe, unshaved and unwashed, and typed steadily for three hours, much like a suicide who never gets around to killing himself because he keeps thinking up new and compelling reasons why he should. I filled nearly ten pages of Hilton stationery and put them into an envelope that I addressed to Myron Greene. I wrote air mail and par avion all over it, mixed a weak whisky and water, and sat there in my bathrobe, thinking about whether what I had written made any sense. I thought about that until it was time to get dressed and go buy back the Sword of St. Louis.

At twenty minutes to three I was pushing a baby buggy containing an attaché case stuffed with £100,000 east on Mount Street toward South Audley Street wondering if, at thirty-eight, I really deserved all those smiles and encouraging nods that came my way.

I dawdled along, arriving at the park at five minutes to three. It was a nice little park with a large iron gate that made it look as if it should be forbidden to the public, but it wasn't. It was shaped like a pot with the handle tapering off east toward Berkeley Square. It had always had a soothing effect on me and I had used it, years ago, as a place to compose myself after a fight with my ex-wife. I had got to know it rather well, there toward the end.

They had her dressed up as a nanny, sitting on the bench that she was supposed to be sitting on, the one that had been donated by the American woman out of gratitude for having been allowed to sit in a public park. The dressed-up nanny's pram, I noticed with a twinge of envy, was bigger than mine, but it would have to be, if it were to hold a sword whose blade was thirty-four-and-a-half inches long.

Her head was turned, but when I pulled up beside her she looked at me and although somebody had dressed her up as a nanny, she didn't look much like one, unless it was the nanny in a blue movie I had once seen. She still wore too much green eyeshadow and I don't think that she had washed her face since I had first seen her, which was when she had opened the door of Tick-Tock Tamil's establishment in Paddington.

"Hello, love," I said. "Is the poor little tyke over his cold yet?"

"You're not clever," she said. "Where is it?"

"In a case under a blanket to keep warm."

The two prams were drawn up side by side. She rose and moved over to mine, bending from the waist as if to peer in at its darling occupant. "Don't try nothing," she said.

"Don't worry," I said and bent over the pram. I pulled back a blanket, a pink one this time, and there it lay, wedged in at an angle. It didn't look like a million pounds or so, but I was no judge. I heard a click then and I looked down. An open switchblade knife was in the girl's right hand.

"Don't try nothing," she said again.

"All you have to do is count up to a hundred," I said. "If you can't go that high, I'll give you a hand."

"Clever bastard," she said and went on counting the £1,000 packets.

172

I took the magnifying glass from my jacket pocket and examined the hilt just below the pommel. There were two tiny scratches there all right, shaped like the letters NN. I took the Polaroid shots from my pocket and compared them with the sword that lay in the baby buggy. They duplicated it in every detail.

I straightened up. "Okay," I said. "I'm satisfied."

She snapped the lid closed on the attaché case with her left hand and drew the blue blanket over it. Her right hand still held the switch blade. "I go first," she said.

"Sure," I said, my eyes on the knife. "I just noticed something though."

"What?"

"You've got rubber baby buggy bumpers."

"You're balmy, you are."

"No," I said, my mouth and throat suddenly dry. "I just wanted to see if I could say it."

She backed slowly away from me, one hand pulling the £52 pride of Harrods, the other holding the open knife down by her side in the folds of her dress that wasn't quite a uniform. When she was about five yards away, she closed the knife and dropped it into the pram. She stared at me for a moment, as if to make sure that I wasn't going to try something tricky. Then she turned the pram around and walked east, pushing her £100,000 toward Berkeley Square.

"Tell Tick-Tock I said hello," I called after her, but she didn't respond, she just kept on walking, her hips swaying a trifle too much for a nanny. Not too much for a Swedish *au pair* maybe, but too much for a proper nanny. I turned and pushed my pram toward South Audley Street, crossed the street, and moved on to Number 57 where the gray Rolls with old Tom at the wheel was waiting in front of Purdey, the gunsmith. I wrapped the sword up in the pink baby blanket as well as I could and climbed into the rear seat, leaving the pram at the curb.

"Everything all right, sir?" old Tom asked.

"It had better be," I said.

173

Chapter
Twenty-Three

*G*entleman Jack Brooks was working the door at the Belgravia mansion that housed the Brothers Nitry and when I asked him what had happened to the Portuguese maids, he said, "Gave them the afternoon off, sir, seeing that it's a private family affair. They're all waiting for you in the red room."

He was right when he had said that they were all there. Eddie Apex was standing in front of the fireplace, gazing up at the fake Eakins. His wife, Ceil, was seated in one corner of the room, about as far away as she could get from Robin Styles who, elegant as ever, sat in a chair in the opposite corner looking relaxed to the point of languidness.

The Nitry brothers, Ned and Norbert, stood in the center of the red room about three feet apart. There was nothing relaxed about them. The jungle was peeking through their Belgravia facades and they both looked ready to pounce.

The man who stood between them didn't look too calm either. He was nervously picking at the crumbs in a plate that appeared to have once held a slice of cake. He was concentrating on getting every last crumb, using his fingers to do so. He was Julian Christenberry, Ph.D., M.A., F.S.A., sage of Ashworth Road, and eminent authority on old swords worth a million pounds or so. He still looked as hungry as ever, but he stopped chewing when he saw the pink-wrapped bundle in my arms.

"You got it, lad!" Ned Nitry said, his voice cracking from excitement or greed or both.

"I got it," I said.

"Put it over here," he said, indicating a long, polished oak table. "Put it over here and let the doctor have a look. You've met the doctor, haven't you?"

"We've met," I said. "How are you, Doctor Christenberry?"

"Mmm," he said, which I interpreted to mean that he was just fine.

I walked over to the table and put the bundle down. I drew back the pink baby blanket and listened to the sigh that ran through the room. They were all crowded about it now. Even old Tom and Gentleman Jack Brooks had tiptoed in and were standing a little to one side. The rest of them looked hungry, famished really, as if they couldn't get enough of the sight of the sword.

"That's it, right enough," Norbert Nitry said.

"Move back so the doctor can have a look," his brother said. "Everybody move back. You need more light, Doctor? Fetch another lamp, Jack."

Everybody moved back and old Jack brought over a floor lamp and plugged it in. It may have been Doctor Christenberry's finest hour and he played it for all it was worth, as if he knew he probably would never command an audience this large again and certainly never one so attentive.

He bent over the sword without touching it until his nose was no more than three or four inches from the tip, which was about as sharp looking as an ordinary carving knife. His nose traveled up the sword until it reached the pommel where the uncut diamond as big as an egg was.

Doctor Christenberry said "Mmm" again, which this time I interpreted to mean that, yes, this object on the table is indeed a sword.

He straightened up and carefully turned the sword over so that he could see what was on the other side. Then his nose began its trip from tip to pommel again. After that he whipped out a tape measure and checked how long it was. Without being told to do so, Norbert Nitry produced a small scale, the accurate kind, the kind that uses polished weights, and Doctor Christenberry weighed the sword. He said "Mmmm" again, meaning this time, I thought, you can take away the scale, which Norbert Nitry did.

Doctor Christenberry stared at the sword as it lay on the polished table. Nobody said anything. The old man reached into his pocket, took out a large hand magnifying glass, and made a careful, minute examination of the blade and then the hilt. When he got to the tiny NN that was scratched into the hilt he said "Mmm" again and let the Nitry brothers have a look. They looked and then grinned at each other.

The old man put the magnifying glass back in his pocket and produced a jeweler's glass. He screwed it into his right eye and made a careful examination of the two rubies that were stuck into both ends of the steel crosspiece. Then he went to work on the big, milky-looking diamond in the pommel. He examined the diamond for nearly five minutes, said "Mmmm" three times, and then unscrewed the jeweler's glass from his eye and dropped it into his pocket. He turned to face his audience.

"This, without doubt," he said and paused, "is the Sword of St. Louis."

I think a faint cheer went up in the room from everyone but Doctor Christenberry and me. Norbert slapped his brother on the back. Eddie Apex embraced his wife. Robin Styles smiled and looked foolishly happy. Old Jack and old Tom did a couple of jig steps. I found myself thinking of Dickens at his stickiest, always toward the end, where good is rewarded and bad is punished, just as in real life.

"Let's have that bubbly now, Jack," Ned Nitry said, beaming, and old Jack went out and came back in wheeling a drinks tray. Ned Nitry moved over to me and put his arm around my shoulder. "I want to thank you, lad, for a damn fine job of work. When would you like your money?"

"You've already paid me twelve hundred and fifty pounds. That was the twelve and a half percent in advance that my attorney asked for."

"That's right. We paid that. And the way I'm feeling now, there just might be a bonus on top of the rest."

"No bonus," I said.

Ned Nitry took his arm from around my shoulder. "No bonus?" he said.

It was as good a time as any. I walked over to the table where the sword still lay. I picked it up by its hilt. It had a nice heft. They had all turned toward me—Eddie and his wife near the door where the drinks tray was; Robin Styles before the fireplace with Norbert Nitry; old Doctor Christenberry by the window, a big glass of sherry already in his hand, probably because it had more nutritive value than champagne; old Tom and Jack hovering around the drinks tray.

With the sword in my right hand, I looked at Ned Nitry who was still standing next to me. "How much do you think this thing will really bring?" I said. "I mean cut out all the crap. What do you think the top price is?"

"What is it, lad?" Ned Nitry said. "Is it a bit more money that you're wanting?"

"No," I said. "I don't want any more money. I just want to know what a realistic price for the thing is."

"Well, why not?" Ned Nitry said. "We're all friends here. We'll all share, even you, lad, if that's what's bothering you. With the way the market is now and inflation and all, why, it'll fetch close to—three million quid."

Still holding the sword in my right hand, but letting the flat of its blade rest against my shoulder, I walked over to the fireplace where Robin Styles stood. "Did you hear that?" I said to him. "Three million pounds. Your cut will be two million. Tax free, or almost. It'll take a long time to lose all that, even with your luck."

"You're going to tip 'em off, the authorities, aren't you, St. Ives?" Ned Nitry said. "All right. If it's only a little blackmail, we don't mind paying, do we?" He looked around the room. He got a nod from his brother. Nobody else nodded. Nobody else said anything.

"I only get paid for what I do," I said.

"Well, you'll get paid for fetching us the sword back. Do you want it now? Is that it? Get him his money, Bert."

"Don't bother," I said. "I didn't earn it."

I was standing by the slate hearth of the fireplace. Slate is an attractive stone, not too hard, easily workable, and makes a right nice roof. I knelt and banged the pommel of the sword down on the slate as hard as I could. The diamond as big as an egg shattered just like a glass doorknob would shatter.

Somebody gasped and then there was a silence. It lasted for five seconds or so while their brains worked, while they figured it all out, while they realized fully what had happened, and who should be blamed.

Then the Nitry brothers, acting in concert without previous consultation, sprang at old Doctor Christenberry and started beating hell out of him.

"You old son of a bitch!" Ned Nitry screamed. "You said it was real! You said it was the goods!" The old man sank to the floor and Norbert Nitry was aiming a kick at his stomach when I pushed him away.

"Leave him alone," I said. "He was bought the way you'd buy a watch. What did you expect? You were talking in millions and he was getting what, a few hundred pounds?"

"It's a fake," Norbert Nitry said, turning from the old man. "It's a goddamned fake." He looked at me. "You could have switched it," he said. "He could've switched it, couldn't he, Eddie?" He turned to look for Eddie Apex, but Eddie wasn't there.

"Where's Eddie?" Ned Nitry demanded. "Where'd Eddie go?"

"He slipped out, sir," old Tom said. "Just before Mr. St. Ives broke the sword. Miss Ceil went after him."

"Get me a drink, Tom," Ned Nitry said. "Whisky. A large one."

"Make it two, Tom, if you don't mind," I said.

With the drink in his hand, Ned Nitry stood in the middle of the room, glaring around, as if trying to decide whom he was going to beat up on next. Finally, he went over to the fireplace and picked up a bit of the smashed glass that had been posing as a diamond.

He looked at it for a moment and then tossed it into the fireplace. I was still holding the sword and wordlessly he stretched out his hand for it. I handed it to him, hilt first. He knelt down and hammered a pea-sized ruby that was stuck into the end of the crosspiece onto the slate. The ruby broke; shattered, really, just like the diamond that had turned out to be glass.

He looked at the sword and shook his head. Then he looked at me. "All faked?" he said.

"All."

Ned Nitry shook his head again, looked around for someplace to put the sword, and then put it in the stand that held the fire tongs and the poker. He put it there idly, as if he never expected to see it again. He walked over to the window where old Doctor Christenberry still knelt on the rug, his head bowed. The old man was making an odd sound and I decided that he was crying again, or trying to, and couldn't quite remember how.

"Who put you up to it, dad?" Ned Nitry said. "Who bought you?"

The old man raised his head. A couple of tears had made tracks down his face where he had forgotten to wash. "I don't know," he said.

"What do you mean, you don't know?"

"It was just a voice. A voice over the telephone."

"A man's voice?"

"Yes, a man's voice."

"What kind of accent, English, American, or what?"

"There was no accent."

"He had to have one or the other."

"I couldn't tell. I tried to, but I couldn't."

"I couldn't either," I said. "It was probably the same guy who called me. I couldn't tell what he was and I tried."

"How much did he pay you, dad?" Ned Nitry said. "How much did he pay you to lie to us?"

"A thousand pounds. He sent it round by taxi in an envelope."

Ned Nitry turned to old Tom. "Get him out of here, Tom."

While Tom was ushering the old man out, Ned Nitry turned to me. "How did you know, goddamnit? How did you know it was faked?"

"I didn't know for sure," I said. "I only suspected because I knew somebody who could have done it. In fact, he probably did."

Ned Nitry got interested. "Who? Who did the fake?"

"A man called Curnutt, but it doesn't matter now. He's dead. He was murdered."

"I read about him," Bert Nitry said. "He was a locksmith, wasn't he?"

"Among other things."

"If you knew it was faked, why didn't you tell us?" Bert said. "Why'd you pay out all that good money, if you knew it was a fake?"

"I didn't know. I only suspected. I didn't really know until I banged it down on the slate. If it had been a real diamond, I'd have looked like a fool, but that's all. The slate wouldn't have hurt the diamond. And as I said, I'd've looked a little like a fool, but not as much like a fool as you would, if you tried to sell it. I figured that there was a fifty-fifty chance that it would be the real thing. The thieves wouldn't deal with an expert—and besides, the only one you had could be bought. So I spent your money. I don't think I made a mistake. I think I gambled and I lost."

"With our money," Ned Nitry said.

"That's right. With your money. So I still have sort of an obligation."

"To do what?" Ned Nitry said.

"To get your sword back. Or rather Styles's sword. You'd like all that lovely money, wouldn't you, Robin?"

"You know damned well I would."

"Good," I said. "Then you can come along and help."

Chapter
Twenty-Four

I had a hard time breaking away from the Nitry brothers because they kept asking me questions for which I had only guesses as answers. Guesses or lies. So I kept telling them I didn't know and that they should ask Eddie and no, I didn't know where Eddie had gone off to sudden like that.

When we finally escaped from the Nitry mansion, Robin Styles and I caught a taxi. I told the driver to take us to the Avis car rental garage off Park Lane.

"What do you need a car for?" Styles said.

"To carry the sword in," I said.

He didn't seem too impressed with what I rented, a Volkswagen, but I had decided that what I needed was anonymous reliability rather than flash and speed. After I signed for the car, I told Robin Styles, "You drive."

He got behind the wheel, checked the brakes, fiddled with the seat adjustment, tested the clutch a couple of times, seemed to check what gauges there were, and we were off. He drove very well, but then he did everything very well, except gamble.

"Where do you want to go?" he said.

"A hardware store," I said.

"A what?"

I had to think a moment to make the translation. "An ironmonger."

He knew of one on Edgware Road so we went there to make my purchases. I bought the largest screwdriver the shop had, a small handsaw, a pair of long-nosed pliers, and a monkey wrench, a request which had the shop assistant puzzled and me resorting to gestures until I remembered the English translation and asked for a spanner. It wasn't all that bad though. I once had spent an entire afternoon trying to find a bottle of rubber cement. I never did find any, nor did I ever learn what the English call it. Elastic gum paste perhaps.

I also bought a cloth bag to carry my new tools in and when we got back to the Volkswagen, I tossed it into the rear seat. "I'm going to walk back to the hotel," I said to Styles. "I'd like you to stay out of sight for the rest of the day. Go take a drive in the country. Find a girl. But stay away from your usual spots. Why don't you just consider yourself as being temporarily in my employ for the next twenty-four hours or so, if you can stand it. Working, I mean."

"It will take some adjustment," Styles said.

"Well, here's fifty pounds to help it along. For expenses. I don't expect an itemized accounting. When you get your three-million-pound sword back, you can buy me a small castle someplace. Maybe in the Cotswolds."

Styles took the fifty pounds and put them into his wallet. He looked at me, then at the bag of tools in back of the VW, and then back at me. "When do we do it?"

"Do what?"

"Burgle whomever you have in mind."

"After midnight," I said. "They tell me it's always better after midnight."

"And you want me to pick you up?"

I nodded. "At the stroke of twelve in front of the Hilton. I'll be the man in the domino mask."

Styles shook his head. "I hope you know what you're doing."

"Mmm," I said and let him interpret that anyway he wanted to.

There were no messages for me at the desk at the Hilton so I went on up to my room and said hello to Ceil Apex who was standing by the window admiring my view of Hyde Park.

She turned slowly. "You don't seem overly surprised."

"I was expecting either you or Eddie."

"And you got me."

"So I did. Would you like a drink?"

"Yes," she said, "I would rather."

I fixed two whiskies with water from the bathroom tap and handed her one. I lifted my glass a little and said, "To the biggest scam of all."

"Eddie's," she said.

"And yours."

"Yes. Mine too."

"Where's Eddie?" I said. "Out trying to patch things up?"

"Something like that."

"And you're here with a proposition."

"A proposal," she said.

"What?"

"Do nothing. Do absolutely nothing for twenty-four hours and Eddie'll have it worked out by then."

"You'll have to do some convincing."

"How?"

"Well, there's your fair body, for instance, although that may be a sexist notion that's gone out of style."

She looked at me coolly with those cat eyes of hers. "If you want it," she said.

"And then there's money. That's always in style."

"We haven't any."

"None at all?"

"We've been stony for nearly a year. Eddie sank every-thing into a couple of ventures that went sour, probably because they were legitimate and he was out of his depth. We've been living off Dad."

"And then the sword turned up."

"Yes. The sword turned up."

"What would Eddie's share have been, if it had all gone the way it was supposed to have gone?"

"Dad and Uncle Bert had agreed to give him the finder's fee."

"Ten percent?"

She nodded.

"So if they made around eight or nine hundred thousand pounds net after expenses out of a three-million-pound deal, he would get ten percent of their profit. About eighty or ninety thousand pounds."

"And we owe that much," she said.

"He would," I said. "So he decided to go for the whole pot."

"We decided."

"Yes," I said. "You both decided. He'd have to have you in on it or he couldn't have used old Jack Brooks and he needed an expert thief to steal the thing, didn't he? Eddie's no thief."

She sighed. "I didn't give poor old Jack much choice really. I told him we'd have to sack him unless he helped us. It was like telling your grandfather to get out, but Jack didn't need much persuasion."

"Then the killing started," I said.

"Eddie had nothing to do with that."

"No?"

"No."

"All right. Who did?"

"We don't know."

"Remember when I called Eddie early that morning and told him I had to go to Highgate? That's all I told him.

That I had to have the one hundred thousand pounds and a ride to Highgate. But when old Tom picked me up, he knew that we had to go to the Swain's Lane entrance. Eddie must have told him. So if Eddie knew that he also knew that the dead man was already tucked up underneath the piano lid out there. You should watch that superannuated help of yours. Their minds wander. They talk too much."

"We had to use what help we could get, and the cheaper the better."

"Such as Tick-Tock Tamil?"

"Yes, we used Tick-Tock to get the name of his man Curnutt. Then we used Curnutt's son to dope your drink."

"I still don't understand that," I said.

She sighed and turned toward the window once more. "We needed the time. Or Curnutt did. It was taking him more time to make the duplicate sword than he had thought. You were already here so it was merely a slight delaying tactic."

"You handled Curnutt, didn't you?"

"What do you mean handled him?"

"I mean that you talked him into it. Persuaded him to make the duplicate sword."

She nodded, her back still to me. "Yes, I persuaded him. I even convinced him that I was going to make certain that the real sword got back to its rightful owner. We even had a code worked out. A torn playing card. He was rather a romantic little man."

"So is Robin Styles," I said. "He believes you, too."

"Another of my assignments," she said. "Robin. Keep Robin happy, I was told. I must say I tried."

"Now you've got another assignment," I said. "Me."

She turned. "Neither Eddie nor I had anything to do with those men being killed."

"And you don't know who did."

"We don't know."

"Crap," I said. "Eddie had it all set. Curnutt would make the duplicate sword and Curnutt's son would return it for the one-hundred-thousand-pound ransom. That was to be their cut and it would also take care of Tick-Tock, wouldn't it?"

"Yes, that was the way it was to have been, originally."

"Then when I brought back the fake sword, Eddie had that old man all bribed up to swear that it was real. Everybody would be happy then, until your father and uncle tried to sell the sword and learned that it was fake. You and Eddie would express a lot of horror and commiseration. But Eddie would have the real sword stashed away someplace and then, maybe a year from now, maybe less, he would make his own deal for the entire amount and split with no one—not Robin Styles, not your uncle or father, no one. The French would never tell who they'd bought it from. That was the way it was supposed to work, wasn't it?"

"Yes. That was the way it was supposed to work."

"And I would even get paid in full for what I did. Your father and uncle would be satisfied that the real sword was delivered to them, the genuine article. They would have old Doc Christenberry's sworn word for it. I would be back in New York spending my money before they ever found out that the sword was a fake. And if they started suspecting me, then that would be just too damned bad as far as you and Eddie were concerned."

"You are rather clever, aren't you?"

"No, I'm not clever," I said. "I just kept stumbling over dead bodies. They always make me think. Or worry. That's what Eddie should have done. Worried a little. Thought a little. He should have thought that a three-million-pound sword might cause people to go around killing other people, especially the people he knows. Where is he now?"

"He's out looking for Tick-Tock."

"Does he know where to look?"

"He thinks so."

"He also thinks that Tick-Tock has the real sword?"

"Yes."

"And that Tick-Tock killed Curnutt and his son?"

"Who else could have?"

"Robin Styles, for one," I said.

Her face changed without her knowing it. Up until then, she had been making it do what she ordered it to: express quiet sorrow, faint irony, weary resignation. Now it expressed surprise and even shock and she almost had to struggle to get it back under control.

"He couldn't have."

I smiled at her. "You really were going to doublecross Eddie, weren't you? You called Curnutt romantic, yet from what I've learned about him, he was about as romantic as a doorknob. But he was religious and I can imagine the cock-and-bull story you fed him about how he should pass the real sword over only to the upright Christian who would come calling for it with the other torn half of the jack of spades. Then what? Then you and Robin Styles were going to ride off into the sunset with a three-million-pound sword that you could peddle as well as your father and uncle could because you knew all their tricks. That was about it, wasn't it?"

She put her glass down and turned back toward the window. "That was it," she said, "but that's not it now. I'm stuck with Eddie. I'm in as deep as he is now."

"And Eddie still trusts you, doesn't he?"

"Yes. He trusts me."

"That's more than I do."

She turned. "What about my proposal? Will you give us our twenty-four hours to patch things over?"

"No."

She stood there looking at me. This time she had slipped on a thoughtful expression. "If you do find the sword, I know where and how we could sell it."

"For three million pounds."

"Yes," she said. "For at least three million pounds."

"Just you and I."

"The two of us."

"There's only one thing wrong with that, honey."

"What?"

"For some reason I don't think I'd live long enough to spend mine."

Chapter
Twenty-Five

*H*ammersmith isn't all that hard to find. You just start heading west and run right into it. But Robin Styles didn't seem to be too sure where it was, so I had to get out a small map and start giving him rights and lefts.

"Don't you ever get out of Mayfair?" I said.

"Certainly, but I don't come here very often. No occasion to, really."

He had picked me up in the Volkswagen promptly at midnight, but because of our wanderings through West Kensington, we didn't pull up in the alley behind 14 Beauclerc Street until nearly one. We coasted up to the back door of the locksmith's shop with our lights and engine off.

I reached into the back seat for my sack of impromptu burglar tools and suddenly remembered one I had forgotten. "Shit," I said.

"What's wrong?"

"I forgot to buy a flashlight."

"Here," Styles said, "I have a pocket torch. One of

these disposable things that you throw away when it burns out."

"You always carry it?"

"No, I bought it late this afternoon. I noticed that you didn't buy one at the ironmonger's, but I didn't want to say anything."

"Thank you. I'm very sensitive."

"Not at all."

Holding my sack of tools in one hand and the small flashlight in the other, I got out of the Volkswagen and went around it to the back door of the locksmith's shop. I was worrying about what tools I should use to pry open the door, especially since it was a locksmith's door. I was also worrying about the murder squad from Scotland Yard and whether they had sealed the door. Homicide does that in New York sometimes. Seals the door. I ran the flashlight up and down the locksmith's door. It wasn't sealed. At least not from the outside.

"What're you doing?" Styles whispered.

"Trying to decide what I should use."

"Mind if I have a look?" he said. "I've locked myself out a few times."

I could see that he was going to be a great help. He took the flashlight and ran it up and down the door, inspected the hinges, and then shined it on the locks. There were three of them. "Hmm," he said and gave the doorknob a tentative sort of try. It turned easily and the door opened.

Robin Styles stood there as if expecting to be congratulated, or maybe even knighted, so I handed him his prize, the monkey wrench.

"I say," he whispered, "what's this?"

"A blunt instrument," I whispered back. "The door's open. That means somebody has gone inside and is, or is not, still there. If the somebody is still there, you may wish to bash him with a blunt instrument."

"I've never done anything like this."

"You virgins are all alike. Here. You can carry the tools, too."

"What do you have?"

I showed him the huge screwdriver, the nearest thing to a legitimate jimmy that the ironmonger had.

"You seem to know the way," he said. "I think you'd better go first."

Well, why not, I thought. The Minnesota Multiphasic Personality Inventory test that I had once taken on a female psychologist's dare showed that I had definite leadership potential. Most people who rate high on the schizophrenic scale do, and she'd said that I was right up there with the best of them, Huey Long, Pancho Villa, George Custer. People like that. The real crazies. But I'd rated very low on paranoia. "That's your trouble," she'd said. "You not only believe that there's nobody out to get you, but you wouldn't give much of a shit if they were."

St. Ives, the born leader, stepped into the workshop of the dead locksmith and shined the light around. Nobody shot at me so I let my breath out and took one in, the first in a long while, it seemed. From the little light that the small torch made, the place looked much the same except for the floor near the anvil. There was no dead body slumped against it at an odd angle, but a thick white chalk mark outlined where it had once lain.

I crossed the shop and this time looked carefully behind the thick tan curtain that separated the work area from where the customers were served. There was nobody there.

"Up the stairs," I whispered to Styles and we went up them slowly, I with my screwdriver, he with his monkey wrench, both of us poised to run like hell if there had been the slightest noise. There wasn't and we came out into the kitchen which, from what I could see, was still as neat and tidy as ever.

I led Robin Styles through the small dining room into

the sitting room. I found myself holding my breath again, but when the light from my flash picked out the Christmas tree, I let it out. It was still there.

"A Christmas tree?" Styles whispered, putting a lot of exclamation into it.

"That's right."

"But it's May."

"Maybe it was always Christmas in his heart," I said and ran the light around the base of the tree. The packages still lay there, but they looked different, and I saw that they had all been unwrapped and then rewrapped by somebody who didn't know too much about wrapping packages. The police, I assumed, looking for clues. I hoped they had found one.

I located a small table and put the flash on it so that its light shined on the tree. "Give me that sack of tools," I said to Robin Styles and he handed them over.

I took out the long-nosed pliers and the saw and squatted down by the tree. I put the pliers down and started sawing away at the tree's lowest branches. When I thought I had sawed enough of them off, I turned my head toward Robin Styles and said, "This thing rests in a big bucket. You hold onto the bucket while I pull."

He knelt down and awkwardly grasped the lips of the big pail or bucket. I could think of no graceful way that he could have done it. I grasped the tree by its trunk and pulled. Nothing happened. I pulled again and metal scraped against the sides of the pail and the base of the tree moved up about six inches. I gave another mighty pull and it was free.

The branches had scratched my face and hands and were making them itch. I lowered the tree until it lay on its side. I picked up the flashlight and shined it on the base of the tree, the part that had been resting in the pail. Billy Curnutt, locksmith, had been a proper craftsman. A section of iron pipe about an inch and a half in diameter looked as if it had been run horizontally through the trunk of the tree. When wedged down into the pail, the pipe would have braced the tree firmly.

I ran the light up the trunk of the tree. Although almost invisible, a thin gray wire was wrapped tightly around the trunk. The wire was almost the same color as the bark of the tree, if a Scotch pine, which is coniferous, has bark, and I suppose it does.

I took the long-nosed pliers and started snipping the wire. Once I had it started it unwrapped easily. Then I held out my hand.

"What do you want?" Styles said.

"The monkey wrench."

I took the wrench and tightened its jaws around the iron pipe that stuck out from the tree. I gave the pipe a tug with the wrench and felt it beginning to unscrew. After a few more tugs with the wrench I could unscrew it with my hand. When it came loose I slipped it off and in the light of the torch the ruby seemed to wink at us.

"It's the bloody sword!" Styles said, forgetting to whisper.

"What did you think I was looking for, the candy canes?"

"It's inside the tree."

"I know it's inside the tree. It just fits. Now you can help get it out."

Styles held the tree's trunk up while I pried off the cap that Curnutt had fashioned to cover the pommel of the sword. He had sawed off a thick section of the tree from the base to form the cap. Then he had sawed off another section, hollowed it out until it was large enough to conceal the sword's hilt. He had then split the tree very carefully far enough up to sheath the entire blade. He had then wrapped the wire tightly enough around the split trunk so that no crack was visible. The two sections of iron pipe, of course, had concealed the sword's crosspiece and had also served as a stout brace to hold the tree upright in the pail. Curnutt had even been so meticulous as to countersink the finishing nails that held the cap onto the base of the tree. He had covered the countersunk holes with plastic wood that had been dyed or colored the same as that of sawed pine.

Although the hilt and the crosspiece were now free, the blade was still inserted in the split trunk. I took the trunk from Styles's hands and said, "You've got a pure heart, pull it out."

He pulled and it slid out easily, as if he were drawing it from its scabbard. He held it up wonderingly and stared at it. "How did you know?" he said.

"You might keep a Christmas tree up through March or even April. But not through May, not unless you want a nine-foot-tall tinderbox in your living room. Curnutt was too careful and too neat for that. He had to be using it for something else and who would ever look inside a Christmas tree?"

"You would," Styles said and there was nothing but admiration in his voice. I can take a compliment as well as anyone. I didn't quite blush. Instead, I said, "Let's get out of here."

"Here," he said, handing me the sword that some people thought was worth three million pounds. "You take it. I'll gather up the tools."

"We should have worn gloves," I said. "I should have thought of a flashlight and I should have thought of gloves. I can see I've got a great future as a second-story man."

"I didn't touch anything except the tree and the pail, did you?"

I tried to think. "The outside doorknob. I think we touched that."

"We can wipe it off on the way out."

Styles led the way to the stairs, carrying the bag of tools and the flashlight. I followed with the sword. At the bottom of the stairs, he stopped, turned, and held the flashlight so that I could see the steps.

I started down the steps and his flashlight wavered.

196

It wavered because a voice said, "Hold it right there, mate." The voice sounded as though it belonged to a gun. It also sounded as though it belonged to Tick-Tock Tamil.

I stopped on the second step from the top. Tick-Tock stepped into the light that came from Styles's torch. Tick-Tock was all dressed up in a black turtleneck sweater and black slacks and black sneakers, looking every inch the well-dressed cat burglar. He also carried a very large flashlight, about two feet long, and a very large pistol, a revolver with a long barrel so that it would shoot straight.

The gun I saw was jammed into Styles's kidney. "All right," Tick-Tock said to Styles. "Move over against the wall there, nice and easy now." Styles moved over until his back was against the wall.

Tick-Tock switched on his giant flashlight and shined the light up at me. It almost blinded me. "Okay, St. Ives," he said. "Now just walk down the stairs, one step at a time, nice and slow."

I didn't argue. I started down the stairs, one at a time, holding the sword at something like port arms. The light still blinded me. I felt for the next step with my left foot, found it, or at least thought I did, and started to move my right foot. But my left foot had lied to me and it slipped off the riser. I started to fall and the only thing I thought of was to get rid of the sword so that I could use my hands to catch myself. I flung it away, but I kept on falling. There was a scream—a long loud scream and then I was at the bottom of the stairs, sitting on the bottom one really, looking down at the face of Tick-Tock Tamil who looked up at me.

Tick-Tock's wrinkled, young-old face was working itself about, the mouth twisting down and then up, the eyes closing and opening. His hands were working, too, I noticed in the light from the torch that Styles still held. Tick-Tock's hands were working on the blade of the Sword of St. Louis which had gone right through him, just below his breast bone. He was trying to pull the sword out, or maybe just trying to make it hurt less. He looked up at me again and said, "It hurts. It hurts bad."

I couldn't think of anything to say or anything to do. So I did nothing. I just sat there on the bottom step and stared down at Tick-Tock. He tried a grin, or maybe it was a grimace, and when he was through with that he said, "I always was an unlucky bastard." Then he died. I knew he was dead because I saw him die and because I could smell him.

"He's dead, isn't he?" Robin Styles said.

"He's dead," I said. I stood up carefully. There was nothing broken, but there was a lot that was bruised. I held out my hand and tried, but I couldn't quite bring myself to do it.

"Here," Robin Styles said, "let me." He planted his left foot firmly on the dead Tick-Tock's chest, wrapped his right hand around the hilt of the sword, and pulled it out. Then he methodically wiped its bloody blade on Tick-Tock's black turtleneck sweater. He did it all with one easy flowing motion, gracefully and well, as he did almost everything. He handed me the sword again. "Here," he said. "I'll drive."

We hurried to the door that led to the alley. It was open. We had left it closed. I used my palm to smear its knob. "Wait a second," I said to Styles. "There may be somebody else out there."

"I'll go first and get the engine started. I left the keys in the ignition. Then you can hop in the other side and we're off."

It sounded like a sensible plan, even to a suddenly deposed leader. Anyhow, it was the only plan there was. Styles dashed for the Volkswagen and got the door open. When the door opened, of course, the interior light came on and somebody shot at him. He had a choice. He could slam the car door shut and duck back into the shop with me, or he could gamble on making it inside the car with the interior light staying on until he got behind the wheel and closed the door.

He gambled on getting into the car and, as always, he was a rotten gambler. Whoever was shooting at him shot three more times, using the interior light of the Volkswagen to aim by. It must have been all the light that was needed because Styles was hit three times.

The first shot seemed to strike him in the shoulder and the second one in the leg. By then whoever was shooting had zeroed in and the third shot slammed into his side. Still on his feet somehow, Styles staggered toward me, then fell back against the car door, closing it, and extinguishing the interior light. Then he started sliding down the outside of the Volkswagen until he landed, with a kind of a plop, in a sitting position on the alley pavement, his back against the car. He held his side as well as he could with one hand because it seemed to hurt the most.

His face was very white in the gloom and I could just see the smile that he made his mouth stretch itself into. And then very casually, he said, "Sorry. I really hate to let a chap down."

Like almost everything else he did, he died well, sitting there, trying not to make a fuss about it.

There was a sound behind me. It was the sound of breaking glass. It was the front door of the shop and somebody was coming through it. The front door was no longer an alternative exit. So I took the only one left.

I dashed for the Volkswagen and threw the sword into the rear seat. At virtually the same time I threw myself headfirst through the car door's open window. It's not as hard to do as it sounds, not if somebody's shooting at you, and that's what somebody was doing at me, although they didn't have the interior light to aim by.

I scrambled around inside on the front seats of the Volkswagen, finally getting myself right side up, but still cursing the gearshift. I hunched over the wheel and started the engine, slammed into first, threw out the clutch, and roared off, as fast as a Volkswagen will go, which really isn't very fast at all.

I glanced in the rearview mirror. About fifteen or

twenty yards behind me I could see a man, his feet spread wide apart. He was crouched down into what might be somebody's notion of what a pistol shooter's position should be. He was crouched next to a low, wide car. It looked like a Jensen, the one that costs more than I like to think about.

He shot once more, but he didn't hit anything. At least he didn't hit me. I was concentrating on what was in front of me now. There was another car parked just at the end of the alley. It was a big car, but it didn't seem to be doing anything. Just as I got to it, I switched on my bright lights, trying to blind anyone who might be inside.

There was a man at the wheel of the car, which I saw was a gray Rolls. It was old Tom, Eddie Apex's chauffeur, and he put a hand up to shield his eyes as I went by.

Chapter
Twenty-Six

*I*f my eight-year-old son ever has children, I can tell them of that May night when, across half of London, I led the man who had once led Fangio for three laps. I needn't tell them how it all ended.

It started well enough, I in my Volkswagen and old Tom at the wheel of the gray Rolls with Eddie Apex beside him on the front seat. At least, I assumed it was Eddie. And behind the Rolls came the Jensen, driven by whoever it was who had killed Robin Styles. I didn't have any friends who drove Jensens. Not in London or anywhere else.

My grandchildren will probably think that I'm lying when I tell them that I drove that Volkswagen halfway across London, as fast as it would go, turning at almost every corner, going the wrong way down one-way streets, climbing up on sidewalks sometimes when it seemed appropriate, and doing all this pursued by about fifty thousand dollars' worth of Rolls-Royce and Jensen, and yet never spotting a cop. Not one. My grandchildren will smile and nod, anxious to be off, and a little embarrassed by the sloppy way that Grandpa wolfs down his milk toast and the equally sloppy way that he lies.

I don't think I ever got that Volkswagen into third gear. I kept it in second, its engine keening into the May night, as I skidded around corners into dimly lighted streets that I had never heard of, streets such as Bute Gardens and Edith Road and Gunterstone Road and May Street and Seedlescomb Road, turning sometimes south and sometimes north, but always east, trying to leave the West End.

I stopped at no stop signs, I slowed at no corners, and I nearly killed myself a dozen or more times. And always behind me, never more than half a block away, was the gray Rolls, old Tom probably driving with one hand while trying to tune in some light traveling music with the other. Behind the Rolls, stuck there like a black leech, was the Jensen, occupied by the man who had a gun that he wanted to shoot me with.

As I spun into Half Moon Street I thought about skidding up to the American Embassy and running up its steps with the Sword of St. Louis clutched in my arms. I also thought about dying halfway up those steps with a bullet in my back. The U.S. Marines would be there, of course, and if they weren't too high on pot, they might help drag my body inside.

By the time I got through with that fantasy I was out of Mayfair and into Shaftesbury Avenue in one of whose shops Robin Styles's father years ago had picked up his three-million-pound sword for twelve-and-six and started the chain of events that had led me to my present mess.

Then I was in Bloomsbury and slithering around Russell Square, if a VW can slither, but going the right way for once on a one-way street, and trying to decide where to go next. South, I decided for no good reason, south across the river to Lambeth or Southwark or even Bermondsey. I wasn't quite sure where Bermondsey was. All I knew about it was that they once sold a lot of leather there.

I cut down Bedford Place to Bloomsbury Square and

then I went due south, cutting back and forth in that rabbit warren of streets that surrounds Covent Garden until I came out on the Strand and turned left. It was a straight stretch and I didn't like that because the Rolls started moving up effortlessly, the way that an ocelot might overtake a tortoise with a touch of emphysema.

So I turned again, a sliding skid of a turn that brought me out onto Lancaster Place and headed straight for Waterloo Bridge. It was a mistake, of course. There were no corners to turn on Waterloo Bridge and it was just what the Rolls and the leechlike Jensen needed if they wanted to box me in at the curb, or even smack up against the bridge railing.

I did the only thing I could do, something that I had once seen done before down in Virginia. I doubleclutched the VW and slammed it into first gear, not quite stripping it. I spun the steering wheel and the VW yawed around and almost went over, but not quite, and then I was heading back in the same direction from which I had come. I was on the wrong side of the bridge now and aiming a twenty-five-hundred-dollar Volkswagen bang on at approximately thirty thousand dollars' worth of Rolls-Royce.

The Rolls would have to give way, of course. Economics dictated it. If it didn't, it would crash into the VW and the tailgating Jensen would smash into the Rolls's rear and there would be the tearing of expensive metal and loud screams and much blood and gore. As I said, economics dictated it. Economics and good sense.

But I forgot who was driving the Rolls. I didn't really forget. I just made the mistake of thinking that I could win playing chicken with a septuagenarian without nerves who had once led Fangio for three laps, and after that had enjoyed the reputation of being the best getaway driver in Soho.

I think old Tom smiled at me through his windshield. I'm still not sure, but I think he did. I was going fifty by then and he was going at least sixty, the Jensen right on his rear bumper, and unless he gave way we were going to run into each other halfway across Waterloo Bridge with a loud smack that would be like hitting a stone wall at 110 miles per hour.

Call me chicken. I spun the VW steering wheel when I did because I wanted to keep on living. Old Tom knew that I did and as I flashed past him I knew that I saw him grin. It is what happens when a rotten amateur goes up against a gifted professional. The amateur loses.

But I had made some gain. They would have to turn around and there was the chance that I could get to the end of the bridge, turn right, and duck into the River Police station before I got shot. Then I could explain all about the old sword with its traces of fresh blood.

It happened then, of course. I ran out of gas. The VW's engine coughed, sputtered, caught again, then coughed once more, a little apologetically, I thought, and then it went out. I remembered that I hadn't checked the gas gauge. I had let Robin Styles do that. Then I had told him to go take a long ride in the country. Or find a girl. I suppose I should have told him to fill up the gas tank, but one can't think of everything.

I remembered then that a Volkswagen has a reserve tank. All you have to do is twist a lever that's down underneath the dash and that cuts into the reserve tank that holds a spare gallon, I think. It only takes a minute or so, but I didn't have a minute. I didn't even have thirty seconds because the Rolls was already backing up. I stopped the coasting Volkswagen, grabbed the sword, jumped out, and ran across the bridge to its west side.

The Rolls kept on backing up until it was well past the VW. The Jensen stayed where it was. I was boxed.

So I stood there and watched Eddie Apex get out of the Rolls and start toward me. When I got tired of watching him I looked at the Jensen. Somebody got out of that, too. He was a big man, huge really. It was Wes Cagle. I should have known. A Jensen would be his kind of car.

They both started walking toward me. Then they started to trot. I took the sword and held it by its hilt with two hands. It was a bastard grip, I remembered being told.

You could wield it with either one hand or two. I thought that they must have had big hands back then.

I saw something appear in Wes Cagle's right hand. It glittered a little, but it wasn't what he had used to kill Robin Styles and shoot at me with earlier. It was a knife, a switchblade, I assumed.

There was no place to run. I could stand and fight, of course, laying about me with the Sword of St. Louis, going for the legs first. I understand that that's how it was done back then. They went for the legs beneath the shields. Or I could surrender.

I started swinging the sword above my head, around and around. I swung twice, then thrice, and on the fourth time I let it go and then I turned and watched because I had never seen three million pounds fall into a river before.

It went up in the air about thirty feet, seemed to hang there longer than it really should have, and then it fell straight down into the black waters of the Thames. It didn't make much of a splash.

I turned back. Eddie Apex was no longer trotting toward me. I had counted on that. He had stopped and there was a rueful smile on his face. He held out his hands, palms forward, and shrugged. For him it was all over.

A good con man is, I think, the ultimate realist. He has to be because he can't afford any illusions in his business. If he has any illusions, especially about the layers of greed that are wrapped around the human heart, then he couldn't be a con man—not a successful one. And when a deal has gone sour and the mark has somehow sniffed the rat, there is nothing for the confidence man and ultimate realist to do but smile and shrug and steal away. There's always another mark halfway down the next block.

So when I tossed three million pounds' worth of sword into the Thames, English Eddie Apex shrugged and accepted his loss because there was nothing else to be done. As an ultimate realist, I don't think that Apex really understood what vengeance meant.

But Wes Cagle was no ultimate realist. He was a one-time professional football player turned professional gambler and professional gamblers are notoriously bad losers, if they think they've been cheated. Wes Cagle didn't just think he had been cheated. He knew it. He had seen me cheat him out of three million pounds by tossing it into the Thames.

He roared first. It was rage, I suppose, and anger and also frustration. Then he started toward me and he came fast, two hundred seventy pounds of six foot seven ex-tight end, moving faster than he had ever moved for Princeton, or for the St. Louis Cardinals, coming straight at me with the switchblade knife held low and down to one side as if he knew that that was exactly where it was supposed to be held, which was something no Princeton man should really know.

I backed up. I couldn't think of anything else to do. I could jump into the Thames, but I don't swim all that well. So I backed up until I couldn't back anymore because the bridge railing wouldn't let me.

Then something streaked past me. It was Eddie Apex, going in low and fast, trying to get under the knife. Cagle saw him and tried to fake him out. Cagle had good moves, but his mind didn't work like Eddie's because Eddie had anticipated the fake. It was what he had learned from life. He hit Cagle low and Cagle went up, all two hundred seventy pounds of him, up high into the air, the way it happens every autumn Sunday afternoon, and the coaches see it and turn their heads away because they really don't want to see how they land.

Wes Cagle landed on the railing of Waterloo Bridge, hung there for a moment, and then went over the side down into the Thames. He screamed all the way down and made a very large splash. After that he didn't scream anymore.

Eddie Apex leaned over the railing and looked down. Then he turned toward me and I saw that he was clutching his stomach. There was blood on his hands. He leaned against the railing of the bridge and then he started sliding down awkwardly, much like Robin Styles had slid down the side of the Volkswagen. Like Styles, Eddie Apex landed in a sitting position with sort of a plop.

I didn't want to watch Eddie Apex die. I didn't want to listen to his last words. I was sick of last words. I didn't want to watch anybody else die that night with a quip on his lips so that he could be remembered as having died well, the way you're supposed to. I knew that when I died, unless it was in my sleep or instantaneously, I would die cursing and screaming and blaming somebody, the doctors probably, and demanding all the sympathy that there was around. That's the way I had come into the world. And that was no doubt the way I would leave it.

The Rolls pulled up alongside and old Tom poked his head out. "Get an ambulance and the cops, Tom," I said.

"Is he hurt bad, sir?"

"I don't know. I think so. The knife got him."

Tom looked as if he wanted to say something else, but he didn't. He turned the big Rolls around and sped off.

I squatted down by Eddie Apex. "How bad is it?" I said.

"Bad. It hurts like hell. Where was it?"

"What?"

"The sword. I never got upstairs at Curnutt's."

"He split his Christmas tree and hid it in there."

"Son of a bitch."

"Who killed him, Cagle?"

"Sure. Killed his son, too. The old man got cold feet and was talking about going to the cops. The son was almost as bad. I tried to talk Wes out of it, but it was no go. He got greedy. They all got greedy."

"I talked to your wife," I said.

"I know. She told me. She got greedier than anybody. We could have worked it with the three swords, if they'd just listened to me."

"What do you mean three swords?"

Eddie Apex made himself grin. "You're not sure now, are you?" he said. "You're not sure which one you tossed into the river."

"What three swords, Eddie?"

207

"There were three swords, not two," he said, still grinning. "Tick-Tock has the third one."

"Tick-Tock's dead."

"When?"

"At Curnutt's. I tripped and the sword went through him."

"No shit?" he said, smiling at the news. Then the blood gushed out of his mouth and like almost everybody else that night, English Eddie Apex died.

There were some other questions that I wanted to ask him, of course. Such as which sword was in the river and which one did Tick-Tock have, and now that Tick-Tock was dead, where was that sword? But Eddie was answering no more questions, so I squatted there beside him with the small crowd that had formed, halfway across Waterloo Bridge, and waited for the ambulance and the cops to arrive.

The cops got there first. They always do.

Chapter
Twenty-Seven

*T*hey didn't exactly deport me. After asking me questions for two days, and not believing half the answers I gave, they mentioned that it might be nice if I were to go on out to Heathrow and catch the next Pan Am flight to New York.

Furthermore, to make sure that I had no trouble finding the airport, they were sending their man Deskins along as guide.

I think William Deskins was the only man in Scotland Yard who believed me. He had sat in on some of the questioning and after that he had conducted his own investigation based partly on the answers that I had given. Now over a drink at the airport he was brooding about some of the questions that still remained unanswered.

"The Nitry brothers had almost never heard of you," he said. "You were a friend of their late son-in-law who dropped by for tea a time or two, but they weren't really sure what line of business you were in."

"And Ceil?" I said.

"Well, according to Ned Nitry, his daughter was so overcome by her husband's death that she had to go abroad for her health and he wasn't really quite sure what country she was visiting, although he expected a postcard any day now and as soon as it arrived, he'd let me know. And good God, no, they didn't know shit about any ancient sword. They'd never heard of it. Furthermore, they weren't interested."

"What about old Tom and Gentleman Jack Brooks? You get anything out of them?"

He shook his head. "Those two old lags? Old Jack went senile on me. He's about as senile as you are. Tom said he was driving his governor along Waterloo Bridge when they spotted this altercation. That's what Tom calls it. Altercation. The governor jumped out to see if he could be of assistance, and the next thing he knows he's stabbed by this American chap which only goes to prove, Tom says, that one should never step into a fight between foreigners."

Deskins was silent for a while as he rubbed his thrusting chin. "Doctor Christenberry," he said finally. "I went to see him, too."

"Is he still hungry?"

"You know what he was doing when I called in? He was sitting there in front of a brand new color telly with the biggest box of chocolates I've ever seen, cramming them into his mouth, and giggling and laughing at this children's program. It was an American program, too. I didn't understand it. There were a lot of strange-looking puppets."

"'Sesame Street'?" I said.

"What?"

"The name of the program. Was it 'Sesame Street'?"

"I remember it was some kind of a street. It looked like a slum. But Christenberry was har-har-haring away at it. He wouldn't turn it off either."

"What did he say?"

Deskins sighed. "He said what his solicitor had told him to say. He said he had been engaged to consult the late

Mr. Apex on a matter of a highly confidential nature, which he could not reveal without the permission of Mr. Apex or his heirs. Well, Eddie Apex's heir is his wife."

"That sounds weak," I said.

"It is, but he's seventy-six years old and God knows what his heart would stand. So what do you want us to do, take him downtown and punch him around a bit until he talks? Besides, I don't think he would tell us anything that you haven't already told us."

"Well, good luck to you," I said.

Deskins nodded. "I wonder where it really is?"

"What, the hundred thousand pounds that the Nitrys paid to ransom that fake sword?"

"Oh, she's got that. Tick-Tock's blond bint that you told us about has got that money all right."

"No trace of her though?"

"We don't even know who she is. Tick-Tock changed his women the way you'd change your sheets. All we know is that she's blond and young and wears too much green eye shadow. There can't be more than a million of them like that in London."

Deskins looked down at his drink and then up at me. "Which one do you think it was?"

"Which one what?"

"Which sword do you think it was that you chucked into the river, the real one?"

I grinned at him. "It's got you, hasn't it? You're hooked. You really think there were three swords, the real one and two fakes."

"You got it from the lips of a dying man, St. Ives."

"I got it from the lips of a man who'd forgotten how to tell the truth. Eddie Apex wasn't comfortable with the truth and I think he wanted to die comfortably and one last con would help."

Deskins shook his head. "I've been thinking about it. He could have used a second fake sword. It would have fitted right in."

"How?"

211

"All right, I'll tell you." He paused to take a swallow of his drink. "Wes Cagle was the one who set it all up to begin with, right?"

"He introduced Robin Styles to Eddie."

"And you think Cagle bowed out after that?"

"Apparently not."

"They had to pay that lad, Robin Styles, fifty thousand pounds, didn't they?"

"That's what Styles told me. The Nitry brothers backed him for that much at the tables."

"And he was unlucky?"

"He wasn't just unlucky. He was a lousy poker player."

"He wasn't that bad," Deskins said.

"Oh," I said. "I see. You leaned on somebody at Shields, did you?"

Deskins nodded. "A couple of the dealers that I've had a little trouble with before and who're in my debt. They had their orders. They were to take young Styles for fifty thousand as quick as they could. It wasn't hard. He didn't play poker too well, as you say."

"So where does the second faked sword fit in?"

"If it had been me, I would have used it to keep Cagle happy. They needed to steal the sword in the first place to make a single copy. Then they were going to return the real sword to the Nitry brothers for the one-hundred-thousand-pound ransom. After that, Eddie would switch the real sword for a faked one. Now guess who was supposed to keep the real sword until it was sold?"

"Cagle," I said.

"Right. So Eddie and his wife planned to pull a double switch. They would hand over to Cagle the second faked sword, keeping the real one for themselves. Except that Eddie's wife, if what you say is true, decided to cross her husband. She went to old Billy Curnutt with that torn jack and her story about how Curnutt shouldn't hand over the sword to anybody except the proper Christian who had the other half of the torn playing card."

"The one that Robin Styles had," I said.

Deskins reached into his pocket and brought out a torn card, half of a one-eyed jack of spades. "They found this on Tick-Tock's body. They didn't know what it was so they turned it over to me."

"You mean Ceil Apex was in with Tick-Tock? I don't believe it."

"She was out to get that sword for herself. She tore two one-eyed jacks, gave one-half to Styles and one-half to Tick-Tock and one-half to Billy Curnutt. I think Tick-Tock was the Christian, as you say, who got to Curnutt first and got the real sword."

"Then what was he doing there that night?"

"He needed the faked sword. He knew that there were two of them and he needed one to turn over to Ceil Apex."

"And he thought she'd think it was real?"

"Long enough for Tick-Tock to disappear with the real one. That's all he needed. Maybe six hours."

"So where's the sword? I mean the real one?"

The look that came into Deskins' eyes was dreamy. "Somewhere in Paddington," he said. "We don't know where Tick-Tock went after he left that place of his where you found him. But it's someplace in Paddington. He never lived anywhere else. Cheap lodgings, probably, maybe even two or three to a room. You know how those coloreds are."

"And that's where you think the real sword is, huh?"

Deskins didn't try to disguise it anymore. I don't think he could have, even if he had wanted to. The greed spread across his face and settled down in his eyes. "It'll turn up," he said.

"Where?"

"Perhaps in Shaftesbury Avenue. Perhaps in the Fulham Road. Perhaps one of those wogs will need some cash one Saturday and flog it down on Shaftesbury Avenue for a quid or two."

"And you've got a new hobby, haven't you?" I said. "Sword collecting."

"That's right," he said. "I've got a new hobby."

I reached into my jacket pocket and took them out and handed them to Deskins. "Here," I said. "These'll help with your new hobby." They were the Polaroid shots of the Sword of St. Louis that Ned Nitry had given me.

He stared at the color photographs and licked his thin lips twice. "So that's what it looks like?" he said. "That's what three million quid worth of old sword looks like."

"That's it," I said.

"You don't believe it, do you? You don't believe that it'll turn up?"

"No. I don't. I believe that it's at the bottom of the Thames in about ten feet of muck. Maybe twenty."

Deskins shook his head. "It'll turn up. It'll turn up one of these days."

"On Shaftesbury Avenue," I said.

"That's right. On Shaftesbury Avenue."

They called my flight then and Deskins stuck out his hand and I shook it. "Well, good luck, St. Ives."

"Pleasant dreams," I said.

Chapter
Twenty-Eight

*E*ddie, the Adelphi apartment-hotel's bell captain, greeted me warmly. "Where you been?"

"London," I said.

"Whadja wanta go there for?"

"To look at the Queen."

"Yeah, well, that lawyer of yours got here earlier, so I let him into your place. I don't figure he'll steal nothing."

"Not enough to worry about anyway."

Myron Greene had lunch ready, all spread out on the poker table. I was touched. He had bought some Filipino beer that I like, some thick roast beef sandwiches, potato salad, and even some Polish dills. "What's the occasion?" I said.

"It's May nineteenth."

"What's May nineteenth?"

"It's the feast day of St. Ives."

"I didn't know you were Catholic, Myron. You don't much look it."

"He's the patron saint of lawyers."

"I didn't know that."

"His emblem is the cat."

"I didn't know that either. And I don't think you did until you looked it up."

"My secretary looked it up actually," Myron Greene said, pouring himself some beer. "After I got that letter of yours, I had her look up St. Louis and while she was at it, I decided to find out about St. Ives."

"Well, thanks for the feast day."

"St. Louis was real enough," Greene said, "but according to a friend of mine at the Metropolitan Museum, his sword is nothing but rumor."

I tried the sandwich. It was excellent. "Well, tell your friend that three million pounds' worth of rumor is lying at the bottom of the Thames. That's just my opinion though. Somebody else thinks it's going to turn up any Saturday now in a secondhand store on Shaftesbury Avenue."

"Maybe you'd better tell me about the rest of it," Myron Greene said. "About what happened after you wrote me that letter."

So I told him and when I was through, he said, "Well, you won nearly as much as your fee would have been. I didn't know you played poker quite that well."

"I don't," I said. "I was betting a cinch hand. That's not real poker because you're not gambling anymore. It's a form of licensed stealing, something like an insurance company. But it's free money, isn't it? The tax people don't have to know about it?"

Myron Greene sighed. "Hand it over, will you? Yesterday I got a call from our friend at the IRS. It seems that Inland Revenue in London has gone to a great deal of trouble to notify Washington of just how much you won. Our friend at IRS thought we'd like to know."

"It really does go with death, doesn't it?" I said. "Taxes, I mean."

Myron Greene shifted in his chair and looked uncomfortable, the way that he always looks when he thinks that I'm going to try to say something profound. "What were you going to do with the money?" he said. "I mean the money that you weren't going to tell the tax people about?"

"I was going to spend it," I said.

"How?"

"I had this fantasy coming back on the plane. I always have fantasies on planes. There's this guy out in Vegas who calls himself Amarillo Slim and is supposed to be the world's champion poker player. Well, in this fantasy I was going to take the money and fly out to Vegas and challenge him for the title."

"That's a good fantasy," Myron Greene said.

"There was only one thing wrong. I couldn't think of what to call myself. I needed something snappy and half-way sinister like Amarillo Slim."

"How about Philosophical Phil?" Myron Greene said.

I told him I would have to think about it.

THE PERENNIAL LIBRARY MYSTERY SERIES

Ted Allbeury

THE OTHER SIDE OF SILENCE   P 669, $2.84
"In the best le Carré tradition . . . an ingenious and readable book."
                                       —*New York Times Book Review*

PALOMINO BLONDE   P 670, $2.84
"Fast-moving, splendidly technocratic intercontinental espionage tale
. . . you'll love it."   —*The Times* (London)

SNOWBALL   P 671, $2.84
"A novel of byzantine intrigue. . . ."—*New York Times Book Review*

Delano Ames

CORPSE DIPLOMATIQUE   P 637, $2.84
"Sprightly and intelligent."
                           —*New York Herald Tribune Book Review*

FOR OLD CRIME'S SAKE   P 629, $2.84

MURDER, MAESTRO, PLEASE   P 630, $2.84
"If there is a more engaging couple in modern fiction than Jane and
Dagobert Brown, we have not met them."   —*Scotsman*

SHE SHALL HAVE MURDER   P 638, $2.84
"Combines the merit of both the English and American schools in the
new mystery. It's as breezy as the best of the American ones, and has
the sophistication and wit of any top-notch Britisher."
                           —*New York Herald Tribune Book Review*

E. C. Bentley

TRENT'S LAST CASE   P 440, $2.50
"One of the three best detective stories ever written."
                                       —Agatha Christie

TRENT'S OWN CASE   P 516, $2.25
"I won't waste time saying that the plot is sound and the detection
satisfying. Trent has not altered a scrap and reappears with all his old
humor and charm."   —Dorothy L. Sayers

Andrew Bergman

THE BIG KISS-OFF OF 1944　　　　　　　　P 673, $2.84

"It is without doubt the nearest thing to genuine Chandler I've ever come across. . . . Tough, witty—very witty—and a beautiful eye for period detail. . . ."　　　　　　　　　　　　　　　　　　　　—Jack Higgins

HOLLYWOOD AND LEVINE　　　　　　　　P 674, $2.84

"Fast-paced private-eye fiction."　　　　　　—San Francisco Chronicle

Gavin Black

A DRAGON FOR CHRISTMAS　　　　　　　P 473, $1.95

"Potent excitement!"　　　　　　　　—New York Herald Tribune

THE EYES AROUND ME　　　　　　　　　P 485, $1.95

"I stayed up until all hours last night reading The Eyes Around Me, which is something I do not do very often, but I was so intrigued by the ingeniousness of Mr. Black's plotting and the witty way in which he spins his mystery. I can only say that I enjoyed the book enormously."
　　　　　　　　　　　　　　　　　　—F. van Wyck Mason

YOU WANT TO DIE, JOHNNY?　　　　　　P 472, $1.95

"Gavin Black doesn't just develop a pressure plot in suspense, he adds uninfected wit, character, charm, and sharp knowledge of the Far East to make rereading as keen as the first race-through."　　—Book Week

Nicholas Blake

THE CORPSE IN THE SNOWMAN　　　　　P 427, $1.95

"If there is a distinction between the novel and the detective story (which we do not admit), then this book deserves a high place in both categories."　　　　　　　　　　　　　　　　　　—New York Times

END OF CHAPTER　　　　　　　　　　　P 397, $1.95

". . . admirably solid . . . an adroit formal detective puzzle backed up by firm characterization and a knowing picture of London publishing."
　　　　　　　　　　　　　　　　　　—New York Times

HEAD OF A TRAVELER　　　　　　　　　P 398, $2.25

"Another grade A detective story of the right old jigsaw persuasion."
　　　　　　　　　　　—New York Herald Tribune Book Review

MINUTE FOR MURDER　　　　　　　　　P 419, $1.95

"An outstanding mystery novel. Mr. Blake's writing is a delight in itself."　　　　　　　　　　　　　　　　　—New York Times

THE MORNING AFTER DEATH　　　　　　P 520, $1.95

"One of Blake's best."　　　　　　　　　　　—Rex Warner

Nicholas Blake (cont'd)

A PENKNIFE IN MY HEART P 521, $2.25
"Style brilliant . . . and suspenseful." —*San Francisco Chronicle*

THE PRIVATE WOUND P 531, $2.25
"[Blake's] best novel in a dozen years . . . . An intensely penetrating study of sexual passion. . . . A powerful story of murder and its aftermath."
—Anthony Boucher, *New York Times*

A QUESTION OF PROOF P 494, $1.95
"The characters in this story are unusually well drawn, and the suspense is well sustained." —*New York Times*

THE SAD VARIETY P 495, $2.25
"It is a stunner. I read it instead of eating, instead of sleeping."
—Dorothy Salisbury Davis

THERE'S TROUBLE BREWING P 569, $3.37
"Nigel Strangeways is a puzzling mixture of simplicity and penetration, but all the more real for that."
—*The Times* (London) *Literary Supplement*

THOU SHELL OF DEATH P 428, $1.95
"It has all the virtues of culture, intelligence and sensibility that the most exacting connoisseur could ask of detective fiction."
—*The Times* (London) *Literary Supplement*

THE WIDOW'S CRUISE P 399, $2.25
"A stirring suspense. . . . The thrilling tale leaves nothing to be desired."
—*Springfield Republican*

Oliver Bleeck

THE BRASS GO-BETWEEN P 645, $2.84
"Fiction with a flair, well above the norm for thrillers."
—*Associated Press*

THE PROCANE CHRONICLE P 647, $2.84
"Without peer in American suspense." —*Los Angeles Times*

PROTOCOL FOR A KIDNAPPING P 646, $2.84
"The zigzags of plot are electric; the characters sharp; but it is the wit and irony and touches of plain fun which make the whole a standout."
—*Los Angeles Times*

John & Emery Bonett

A BANNER FOR PEGASUS   P 554, $2.40

"A gem! Beautifully plotted and set. . . . Not only is the murder adroit and deserved, and the detection competent, but the love story is charming."   —Jacques Barzun and Wendell Hertig Taylor

DEAD LION   P 563, $2.40

"A clever plot, authentic background and interesting characters highly recommended this one."   —*New Republic*

THE SOUND OF MURDER   P 642, $2.84

The suspects are many, the clues few, but the gentle Inspector ferrets out the truth and pursues the case to its bitter and shocking end.

Christianna Brand

GREEN FOR DANGER   P 551, $2.50

"You have to reach for the greatest of Great Names (Christie, Carr, Queen . . .) to find Brand's rivals in the devious subtleties of the trade."   —Anthony Boucher

TOUR DE FORCE   P 572, $2.40

"Complete with traps for the over-ingenious, a double-reverse surprise ending and a key clue planted so fairly and obviously that you completely overlook it. If that's your idea of perfect entertainment, then seize at once upon *Tour de Force*."   —Anthony Boucher, *New York Times*

James Byrom

OR BE HE DEAD   P 585, $2.84

"A very original tale . . . Well written and steadily entertaining."
—Jacques Barzun and Wendell Hertig Taylor, *A Catalogue of Crime*

Henry Calvin

IT'S DIFFERENT ABROAD   P 640, $2.84

"What is remarkable and delightful, Mr. Calvin imparts a flavor of satire to what he renovates and compels us to take straight."

—Jacques Barzun

Marjorie Carleton

VANISHED   P 559, $2.40

"Exceptional . . . a minor triumph."
—Jacques Barzun and Wendell Hertig Taylor, *A Catalogue of Crime*

George Harmon Coxe

MURDER WITH PICTURES — P 527, $2.25

"[Coxe] has hit the bull's-eye with his first shot."

—New York Times

Edmund Crispin

BURIED FOR PLEASURE — P 506, $2.50

"Absolute and unalloyed delight."

—Anthony Boucher, New York Times

Lionel Davidson

THE MENORAH MEN — P 592, $2.84

"Of his fellow thriller writers, only John Le Carré shows the same instinct for the viscera." *—Chicago Tribune*

NIGHT OF WENCESLAS — P 595, $2.84

"A most ingenious thriller, so enriched with style, wit, and a sense of serious comedy that it all but transcends its kind."

—The New Yorker

THE ROSE OF TIBET — P 593, $2.84

"I hadn't realized how much I missed the genuine Adventure story . . . until I read *The Rose of Tibet*." *—Graham Greene*

D. M. Devine

MY BROTHER'S KILLER — P 558, $2.40

"A most enjoyable crime story which I enjoyed reading down to the last moment." *—Agatha Christie*

Kenneth Fearing

THE BIG CLOCK — P 500, $1.95

"It will be some time before chill-hungry clients meet again so rare a compound of irony, satire, and icy-fingered narrative. *The Big Clock* is . . . a psychothriller you won't put down." *—Weekly Book Review*

Andrew Garve

THE ASHES OF LODA — P 430, $1.50

"Garve . . . embellishes a fine fast adventure story with a more credible picture of the U.S.S.R. than is offered in most thrillers."

—New York Times Book Review

THE CUCKOO LINE AFFAIR — P 451, $1.95

". . . an agreeable and ingenious piece of work." *—The New Yorker*

A HERO FOR LEANDA P 429, $1.50

"One can trust Mr. Garve to put a fresh twist to any situation, and the ending is really a lovely surprise." —*Manchester Guardian*

MURDER THROUGH THE LOOKING GLASS P 449, $1.95

". . . refreshingly out-of-the-way and enjoyable . . . highly recommended to all comers." —*Saturday Review*

NO TEARS FOR HILDA P 441, $1.95

"It starts fine and finishes finer. I got behind on breathing watching Max get not only his man but his woman, too." —*Rex Stout*

THE RIDDLE OF SAMSON P 450, $1.95

"The story is an excellent one, the people are quite likable, and the writing is superior." —*Springfield Republican*

Michael Gilbert

BLOOD AND JUDGMENT P 446, $1.95

"Gilbert readers need scarcely be told that the characters all come alive at first sight, and that his surpassing talent for narration enhances any plot. . . . Don't miss." —*San Francisco Chronicle*

THE BODY OF A GIRL P 459, $1.95

"Does what a good mystery should do: open up into all kinds of ramifications, with untold menace behind the action. At the end, there is a bang-up climax, and it is a pleasure to see how skilfully Gilbert wraps everything up." —*New York Times Book Review*

FEAR TO TREAD P 458, $1.95

"Merits serious consideration as a work of art." —*New York Times*

Joe Gores

HAMMETT P 631, $2.84

"Joe Gores at his very best. Terse, powerful writing—with the master, Dashiell Hammett, as the protagonist in a novel I think he would have been proud to call his own." —*Robert Ludlum*

C. W. Grafton

BEYOND A REASONABLE DOUBT P 519, $1.95

"A very ingenious tale of murder . . . a brilliant and gripping narrative." —*Jacques Barzun and Wendell Hertig Taylor*

C. W. Grafton (cont'd)

THE RAT BEGAN TO GNAW THE ROPE P 639, $2.84
"Fast, humorous story with flashes of brilliance."

—*The New Yorker*

Edward Grierson

THE SECOND MAN P 528, $2.25
"One of the best trial-testimony books to have come along in quite a while." —*The New Yorker*

Bruce Hamilton

TOO MUCH OF WATER P 635, $2.84
"A superb sea mystery. . . . The prose is excellent."
—Jacques Barzun and Wendell Hertig Taylor, *A Catalogue of Crime*

Cyril Hare

DEATH IS NO SPORTSMAN P 555, $2.40
"You will be thrilled because it succeeds in placing an ingenious story in a new and refreshing setting. . . . The identity of the murderer is really a surprise." —*Daily Mirror*

DEATH WALKS THE WOODS P 556, $2.40
"Here is a fine formal detective story, with a technically brilliant solution demanding the attention of all connoisseurs of construction."
—Anthony Boucher, *New York Times Book Review*

AN ENGLISH MURDER P 455, $2.50
"By a long shot, the best crime story I have read for a long time. Everything is traditional, but originality does not suffer. The setting is perfect. Full marks to Mr. Hare." —*Irish Press*

SUICIDE EXCEPTED P 636, $2.84
"Adroit in its manipulation . . . and distinguished by a plot-twister which I'll wager Christie wishes she'd thought of." —*New York Times*

TENANT FOR DEATH P 570, $2.84
"The way in which an air of probability is combined both with clear, terse narrative and with a good deal of subtle suburban atmosphere, proves the extreme skill of the writer." —*The Spectator*

TRAGEDY AT LAW P 522, $2.25
"An extremely urbane and well-written detective story."

—*New York Times*

Cyril Hare (cont'd)

UNTIMELY DEATH P 514, $2.25
"The English detective story at its quiet best, meticulously underplayed, rich in perceivings of the droll human animal and ready at the last with a neat surprise which has been there all the while had we but wits to see it." —*New York Herald Tribune Book Review*

THE WIND BLOWS DEATH P 589, $2.84
"A plot compounded of musical knowledge, a Dickens allusion, and a subtle point in law is related with delightfully unobtrusive wit, warmth, and style." —*New York Times*

WITH A BARE BODKIN P 523, $2.25
"One of the best detective stories published for a long time." —*The Spectator*

Robert Harling

THE ENORMOUS SHADOW P 545, $2.50
"In some ways the best spy story of the modern period. . . . The writing is terse and vivid . . . the ending full of action . . . altogether first-rate." —Jacques Barzun and Wendell Hertig Taylor, *A Catalogue of Crime*

Matthew Head

THE CABINDA AFFAIR P 541, $2.25
"An absorbing whodunit and a distinguished novel of atmosphere." —Anthony Boucher, *New York Times*

THE CONGO VENUS P 597, $2.84
"Terrific. The dialogue is just plain wonderful." —*Boston Globe*

MURDER AT THE FLEA CLUB P 542, $2.50
"The true delight is in Head's style, its limpid ease combined with humor and an awesome precision of phrase." —*San Francisco Chronicle*

M. V. Heberden

ENGAGED TO MURDER P 533, $2.25
"Smooth plotting." —*New York Times*

James Hilton

WAS IT MURDER? P 501, $1.95
"The story is well planned and well written." —*New York Times*

S. B. Hough

DEAR DAUGHTER DEAD P 661, $2.84
"A highly intelligent and sophisticated story of police detection . . . not to be missed on any account." —Francis Iles, *The Guardian*

SWEET SISTER SEDUCED P 662, $2.84
In the course of a nightlong conversation between the Inspector and the suspect, the complex emotions of a very strange marriage are revealed.

P. M. Hubbard

HIGH TIDE P 571, $2.40
"A smooth elaboration of mounting horror and danger."
—*Library Journal*

Elspeth Huxley

THE AFRICAN POISON MURDERS P 540, $2.25
"Obscure venom, manical mutilations, deadly bush fire, thrilling climax compose major opus.... Top-flight."
—*Saturday Review of Literature*

MURDER ON SAFARI P 587, $2.84
"Right now we'd call Mrs. Huxley a dangerous rival to Agatha Christie." —*Books*

Francis Iles

BEFORE THE FACT P 517, $2.50
"Not many 'serious' novelists have produced character studies to compare with Iles's internally terrifying portrait of the murderer in *Before the Fact,* his masterpiece and a work truly deserving the appellation of unique and beyond price." —Howard Haycraft

MALICE AFORETHOUGHT P 532, $1.95
"It is a long time since I have read anything so good as *Malice Aforethought,* with its cynical humour, acute criminology, plausible detail and rapid movement. It makes you hug yourself with pleasure."
—H. C. Harwood, *Saturday Review*

Michael Innes

APPLEBY ON ARARAT P 648, $2.84
"Superbly plotted and humorously written." —*The New Yorker*

APPLEBY'S END P 649, $2.84
"Most amusing." —*Boston Globe*

THE CASE OF THE JOURNEYING BOY   P 632, $3.12
"I could see no faults in it. There is no one to compare with him."
—*Illustrated London News*

DEATH ON A QUIET DAY   P 677, $2.84
"Delightfully witty."   —*Chicago Sunday Tribune*

DEATH BY WATER   P 574, $2.40
"The amount of ironic social criticism and deft characterization of scenes and people would serve another author for six books."
—Jacques Barzun and Wendell Hertig Taylor

HARE SITTING UP   P 590, $2.84
"There is hardly anyone (in mysteries or mainstream) more exquisitely literate, allusive and Jamesian—and hardly anyone with a firmer sense of melodramatic plot or a more vigorous gift of storytelling."
—Anthony Boucher, *New York Times*

THE LONG FAREWELL   P 575, $2.40
"A model of the deft, classic detective story, told in the most wittily diverting prose."   —*New York Times*

THE MAN FROM THE SEA   P 591, $2.84
"The pace is brisk, the adventures exciting and excitingly told, and above all he keeps to the very end the interesting ambiguity of the man from the sea."   —*New Statesman*

ONE MAN SHOW   P 672, $2.84
"Exciting, amusingly written . . . very good enjoyment it is."
—*The Spectator*

THE SECRET VANGUARD   P 584, $2.84
"Innes . . . has mastered the art of swift, exciting and well-organized narrative."   —*New York Times*

THE WEIGHT OF THE EVIDENCE   P 633, $2.84
"First-class puzzle, deftly solved. University background interesting and amusing."   —*Saturday Review of Literature*

Mary Kelly

THE SPOILT KILL   P 565, $2.40
"Mary Kelly is a new Dorothy Sayers. . . . [An] exciting new novel."
—*Evening News*

Lange Lewis

THE BIRTHDAY MURDER P 518, $1.95
"Almost perfect in its playlike purity and delightful prose."
—Jacques Barzun and Wendell Hertig Taylor

Allan MacKinnon

HOUSE OF DARKNESS P 582, $2.84
"His best . . . a perfect compendium."
—Jacques Barzun and Wendell Hertig Taylor, *A Catalogue of Crime*

Frank Parrish

FIRE IN THE BARLEY P 651, $2.84
"A remarkable and brilliant first novel. . . . entrancing."
—*The Spectator*

SNARE IN THE DARK P 650, $2.84
The wily English poacher Dan Mallett is framed for murder and has to confront unknown enemies to clear himself.

STING OF THE HONEYBEE P 652, $2.84
"Terrorism and murder visit a sleepy English village in this witty, offbeat thriller." —*Chicago Sun-Times*

Austin Ripley

MINUTE MYSTERIES P 387, $2.50
More than one hundred of the world's shortest detective stories. Only one possible solution to each case!

Thomas Sterling

THE EVIL OF THE DAY P 529, $2.50
"Prose as witty and subtle as it is sharp and clear. . .characters unconventionally conceived and richly bodied forth . . . . In short, a novel to be treasured." —Anthony Boucher, *New York Times*

Julian Symons

THE BELTING INHERITANCE P 468, $1.95
"A superb whodunit in the best tradition of the detective story."
—August Derleth, *Madison Capital Times*

BOGUE'S FORTUNE P 481, $1.95
"There's a touch of the old sardonic humour, and more than a touch of style." —*The Spectator*

Henry Kitchell Webster

WHO IS THE NEXT?   P 539, $2.25

"A double murder, private-plane piloting, a neat impersonation, and a delicate courtship are adroitly combined by a writer who knows how to use the language."   —Jacques Barzun and Wendell Hertig Taylor

John Welcome

GO FOR BROKE   P 663, $2.84

A rich financier chases Richard Graham half 'round Europe in a desperate attempt to prevent the truth getting out.

RUN FOR COVER   P 664, $2.84

"I can think of few writers in the international intrigue game with such a gift for fast and vivid storytelling."

—*New York Times Book Review*

STOP AT NOTHING   P 665, $2.84

"Mr. Welcome is lively, vivid and highly readable."

—*New York Times Book Review*

Anna Mary Wells

MURDERER'S CHOICE   P 534, $2.50

"Good writing, ample action, and excellent character work."

—*Saturday Review of Literature*

A TALENT FOR MURDER   P 535, $2.25

"The discovery of the villain is a decided shock."   —*Books*

Charles Williams

DEAD CALM   P 655, $2.84

"A brilliant tour de force of inventive plotting, fine manipulation of a small cast and breathtaking sequences of spectacular navigation."

—*New York Times Book Review*

THE SAILCLOTH SHROUD   P 654, $2.84

"A fine novel of excitement, spirited, fresh and satisfying."

—*New York Times*

THE WRONG VENUS   P 656, $2.84

Swindler Lawrence Colby and the lovely Martine create a story of romance, larceny, and very blunt homicide.

Edward Young

THE FIFTH PASSENGER   P 544, $2.25
"Clever and adroit . . . excellent thriller. . . ."   —*Library Journal*

If you enjoyed this book you'll want to know about
THE PERENNIAL LIBRARY MYSTERY SERIES

Buy them at your local bookstore or use this coupon for ordering:

Qty	P number	Price
_____	_____	_____
_____	_____	_____
_____	_____	_____
_____	_____	_____
_____	_____	_____
_____	_____	_____
_____	_____	_____
_____	_____	_____
_____	_____	_____
_____	_____	_____
_____	_____	_____
_____	_____	_____
_____	_____	_____
_____	_____	_____

postage and handling charge $1.00
_____ book(s) @ $0.25   _____

TOTAL   [＿＿＿＿＿]